# Lady in Red

## Mel Teshco

 **MEL TESHCO**

Lady in Red
©Copyright 2021 Mel Teshco

**Acknowledgements**

Thanks to all the readers who enjoy my stories. Without you I wouldn't be doing this writing gig that I love so much! And thank you to my family for their amazing patience while I lose myself in my imagination, I seriously love you guys to bits!

# Chapter One

**B**randy Alexander, also known as Kate Matthews in her non-fantasy life, stepped out of the chauffeured town car that had collected her. Checking that her upswept hair was still in order, she smoothed a hand down her tiny, crimson leather dress.

Perfect.

Clutch bag firmly in hand, which carried the essential tools of her trade—condoms, lube, lipstick, hairpins and a cell phone, she waited until the car slid away into the night. When its taillights disappeared around a bend, she stepped toward the townhouse with its familiar red front door.

The heels of her thigh-high boots clacked on the granite walkway that led to where her regular client waited. She licked her lips. Blaine Leo Waymann, thirty-six years young and already a billionaire businessman and philanthropist. Not to mention voted "Australia's Bachelor of the Year" three years running by *Cleo* magazine readers.

He could have had any woman he wanted, yet he'd asked specifically for her.

Lord only knew there were enough beautiful women at the VIP Escort Agency, where she worked. Savannah, with her slender body, exotic sloe-brown eyes and black-as-night hair. Tiffany, with her gorgeous silver-blonde locks and ice-blue eyes. Or perhaps Scarlet, with her flame-red hair and pale-as-lily skin.

A smile spread over Brandy's face, melting the distant echo of insecurities clean away. This was why she loved her work. This was why she couldn't give it up any time soon. She would never underrate the value of being wanted, even if it was only for one night.

Her breath puffed in the chill night air, but she barely felt the cold. Excitement warmed her blood until she wondered if she was flushed all over.

Hot, and past ready to be fucked.

Dozens of tiny, discreet garden lights chased away the shadows. Brandy smiled. She could probably walk this too-familiar path blindfolded.

She turned the doorknob, aware it wouldn't be bolted.

She was expected.

Shutting the door behind her before routinely flicking its lock, she turned back to take in the expansive entryway. Marble floors and stark, white spaciousness.

Blaine had requested that she always wear red, and she often wondered if she was his one smoldering flame in an otherwise clean-cut and conventional existence. He was a generous and considerate lover, his skill and passion between the sheets indisputable.

He looked after those in his care. She had no doubt it was for his guests' safety that he had a bodyguard or two stationed around the perimeter of his Sydney home. The same residence that, until recently, he'd occupied only sporadically.

He'd been a regular client, but his appointments with her had steadily increased. His fixation with her was becoming a habit. But she knew his type. He wanted what he couldn't have. He'd offer her the moon, and if she accepted, the game would pall and his obsession would wane.

Her chin tilted as she squared her shoulders. She wasn't in the business of having men lose interest in her.

She sashayed into the living room, with its vaulted ceiling and plush cream carpet. Faint notes of Vivaldi echoed through surround sound speakers, making her entrance somehow even more surreal than usual.

Blaine had eclectic tastes, and Brandy never really knew what to expect. Their every encounter had her gut coiled, as if it was a spring, and her body fueled with hot anticipation.

Going by tonight's music, it seemed his mood was deep. Passionate. Intense.

The loud clink of ice drew her toward the adjacent room he used for entertaining. But her attention wasn't on the bar and its upside-down bottles, or the dancing flames behind a glass domed fireplace.

She had eyes only for Blaine.

He'd recently had a shower, a white towel slung low on his hips and his dark hair almost inky black with moisture. With his back to her, she could afford to drink him in, appraise his athletic, toned body and olive skin, thanks to some distant Spanish heritage.

She swallowed hard as he pivoted to face her. His smile was a lazy quirk of his lips, a vivid contrast to the darkly sinful glint in his brilliant, gold-brown stare. He stepped toward her, dwarfing her even in her ludicrously high heels. Proffering a squat glass with ice and something alcoholic, he drawled, "Beautiful as always."

The compliment never failed to charm. Her past never quite forgotten.

She dropped her bag onto the nearest sofa before accepting the drink. Arching a brow, she retorted boldly, "Fuckable as always."

His husky laugh sent shivers all the way to her toes. She tipped back her drink and swallowed it in one hit. She sighed, relishing the slow whiskey burn that only accentuated the intense chemistry between them. She raised her glass that clinked with nothing but ice. "No brandy tonight?" He always had one ready for her in honor of her namesake.

"Later," he promised. He nodded toward her empty glass and asked, "Would you care for another?"

She arched a brow and said sweetly, "If I didn't know any better, I'd think you were trying to take advantage of me."

His eyes gleaming, he spread his arms out as if in supplication, his drink untouched in one hand. "Would you prefer to take advantage of me?"

With a smile she stepped forward, their bodies all but touching when she handed him her glass. She slid an arm around his nape, and her other hand slipped beneath his towel. His breath hissed as she skated one long nail along the thickening, silky ridge of his shaft before she cupped the heavy weight of his balls in her palm. "Like this?" she asked.

His stare held hers, hot and assessing. "I'm not complaining."

She nodded in the direction of their glasses. "How long do you think you can hold those?"

He raised his arms to shoulder level, the ice clinking in his untouched drink. "As long as needed." His eyes burned with desire. "I'm up for the challenge."

She dropped her hand from between his thighs, wondering if her smile had made it to her eyes. She took these challenges seriously, just the same as he did. But it was even more arousing knowing that Blaine was used to being the one in control. She looked up and held his stare as she reached up and dipped a finger into his untouched whiskey. "Good."

Her hand returned under his towel and she caressed the head of his hard cock with a wet finger, smearing whiskey into his slit. It had to burn, but the pain evidently balanced precariously with pleasure, as he closed his eyes for a moment on a barely audible groan.

When his silky, long lashes flicked back open, his stare alight with desire, she felt a moment of empowerment, knowing he was all but constrained by the glasses in his hands.

"You'll pay for that," he whispered throatily, his eyes glinting. "My god, you'll pay."

She shivered. The scenario was akin to releasing the locks to a tiger's cage and standing back to wait for the inevitable. But then Blaine could never be accused of being boring, especially not in the bedroom. Her hands moved to his ass cheeks, her long nails digging deep enough to hurt when she asked silkily, "Is that a threat or a promise?"

The glasses wavered just a little in his grip. She could have purred with delight.

"It's whatever you want it to be," he drawled, "times ten."

Her breath hitched. Triumph mingled with trepidation. His promised retribution just might be the icing on the cake, if it wasn't for repressed self-doubt suddenly rearing its head. Even now, many years after the bullying and teasing from her peers, she had to remind herself that she was beautiful and desirable. It took the admiration and high regard of men like Blaine to remind her, without so many words, that she was no longer the insecure girl she'd once been.

Her hands moved upward and flattened onto his chest. She stood on tiptoes, her mouth pressing over his before she touched the seam of his lips with her tongue. His growl morphed into a groan when she pushed her tongue into his mouth and rocked against him, emulating the act he paid top dollar for her to carry out.

God, she loved the taste of him. Hot spices and contrary overtones of cool mint. But she needed to slow things down, draw out the moment. She pulled back and licked her lower lip. His eyes narrowed, following the movement.

Dipping her finger back into the glass of whiskey, she swirled a wet trail over one of his nipples, then the other. He sucked in a breath when she leaned forward and licked each trail dry. Faint notes of soap and warm, spiced male teased her nostrils as his already hard nipples became stiff little peaks, his chest rising and falling sharply beneath her hands.

His nipples were his erogenous zones. But with their every encounter, she varied the seduction, mixed it up to make sure her next visit wouldn't be her last.

As a high-class call girl, this night alone would secure her more money than what most people would earn in a handful of months. Except the money had become only a small incentive to keep her in the business. She could afford now to be choosy, her clients predominantly a select half dozen.

She'd discovered a love for sex later in life than most girls. But unlike many of her "friends," she'd gotten off on the empowerment that came with fucking a man senseless. The most influential of men had become completely undone by the thrill of paid sexual release while she...she had been brought to life, a goddess who'd found her calling.

She looked up, holding Blaine's stare as she suckled one of his nipples. A muscle in his jaw throbbed, undoubtedly in sync to the throbbing of his cock.

*Only one way to find out.*

Working her way downward, she pressed kisses over his delicious, silken warm skin, the hard lines of his torso and abs. Regular boxing, jujitsu and aikido bouts apparently kept him honed and strong. And she could certainly attest to his bedroom prowess and stamina.

Unlike her other clients, Blaine had been open about his life. With each encounter, she'd learned a bit more about him. Little things that drew a bigger picture about him, the man.

He was partial to cats, though he had no time in his life right now to own one. Brussels sprouts and liver were never on his menu, while old-fashioned pot roast and roasted vegetables were regular fare. And sex. He loved sex. Lots of it. But she had a strong feeling he'd be faithful once he was attached. Whoever was fortunate enough to keep his bed warm was one lucky woman indeed.

She ignored the unwelcome flash of envy by pushing further thought aside and concentrating on her client.

She stopped at his clenched belly to dip her tongue into his navel and swirl around its rim. His breath rushed out. But it wasn't until she kneeled, untied the knotted towel at his hips before taking his steel-hard cock into her mouth, that his eyes slid closed and his head rocked back.

"Sweet Jesus," he groaned, "I don't pay you nearly enough."

They both knew he could get it for free anytime he wanted, but who was she to argue the point? Even if she hadn't left poverty behind her many years ago, her aphrodisiac would still be the man behind the money. Blaine was clearly focused and driven to have climbed the ladder of success at such a young age, and she found that a turn-on all of its own.

The head of his cock hit the back of her throat before she slowly retreated, suckling hard as, inch by long inch, his shaft withdrew. She swirled her tongue around the head of his cock, lapping up the sticky, salty essence of his pre-cum, before his hips drove forward. With his cock pushed into the back of her mouth, he reversed the thrust, taking up a rhythm that was as decadent and primal as the taste of his essence.

She grazed delicate teeth along his hard, veined shaft. His deep groans intensified until she wondered how he hadn't yet exploded into her mouth.

He abruptly withdrew. Then, depositing their glasses with a sharp clank onto a nearby occasional table, he took her hand and helped her to her feet. All the while, his eyes burned with a dangerous intensity that somehow suited the music wafting from the speakers. Violins sparkled into a crescendo, like a wave rushing across a shore.

"Much as I'm all too tempted to spill into your mouth, I want more from you...much more," he said.

"Intercourse?" she asked, aware that he appreciated her dry sense of humor. Then again, he seemed to appreciate her in any guise.

*He's never seen me slouching around in sweats and a favorite old t-shirt.*

His smile almost disarmed her, had her again momentarily yearn to be something more than his...what? Love toy? Expensive lay?

What would it be like to be someone permanent in his life? Someone he came home to every night?

She bit into her bottom lip to bring her mind back to the present. *Stupid girl.* What was wrong with her? Where were these thoughts coming from? She'd never questioned her life before, never wished for anything more.

At least, not since she'd been a naïve young girl imagining the kind of future many women her age lived for real. But there was no point wondering about the hundred different what-might-have-been scenarios. She'd long ago embraced her chosen career.

She cleared her face as Blaine's brilliant eyes assessed her, seemingly reading her every thought...her every doubt. Then he smiled a little. "Intercourse...yes, if that's what you want to call it." With her hand still in his, he brought her farther into the room. "I've got just the place."

Something beyond excitement shuddered through her body. "Oh?"

He stilled behind a sofa, bringing her to his front so that she could see their reflection in the huge wall mirror. Her strawberry-blonde hair should have clashed with her flame-red dress. It didn't. Better yet, the colors were a dramatic foil to his dark coloring, the fire to his night.

His eyes glinted with wicked intent. "I want you to watch while I make you come."

His head dropped low. She gasped when he raked splayed hands through her hair and tugged her back.

*Oh god.*

Her scalp burned a little at the pressure. But his mouth burned hotter still across her throat, sending a lightning bolt of need through her nerve endings, and a flood of moisture straight to her pussy.

It was beyond erotic to watch him take control, his expertise obvious and his restraint somehow sexy. His large hands moved down the bodice of her dress and cupped her breasts. Without the restriction of a bra, his thumbs all too easily caressed her already hard nipples into sharp little points.

His dark head moved slowly, luxuriously up her nape. When he took her earlobe into his mouth and suckled, she arched into him on a groan, a round of shivers rippling through her body.

She could only be glad his big body was behind her, supporting her weakened knees. Right now, she could barely function beyond the most basic level of awareness. Perhaps that was why she didn't at first notice that he'd moved his hands from her breasts to take hold of her front zipper?

Soft, cool air caressed her bared skin. The hot, hard throb of his cock pressed against the small of her back. She dropped her arms and Blaine stepped back for a beat, her dress sliding free from her shoulders and landing on the floor in a whisper of sound. Leaving her in a barely there, lacy, crimson thong.

"Dance for me," he rasped in her ear.

Taking her cue from the violins, she slithered down, against his hardness, then back up again. Her eyes glinted back at her in the mirror as she coiled her arms above her head, her hips sashaying to the magical notes pulsing through the room. She reached back and clasped his nape, bringing him nearer still.

On a heavily exhaled breath, he reciprocated, trailing kisses once again down her throat and suckling at her flesh while she gyrated against him. Her lips parted and her eyelids fluttered half shut as a furnace of heat built inside her.

Some kind of expletive, that sounded much like a benediction, filled her ears. Then his legs kicked apart so that he was spread-eagle behind her, and eye-level to her in the mirror. His cock slid between her ass cheeks and4 glanced over her aching clit. She gasped. With only her flimsy lace thong as a barrier, nerve endings flared into life, pooling warmth between her thighs.

He pushed a hand down the front of her thong, using a finger to probe between the slick folds of her flesh. "You're so wet for me."

That was a gross understatement. But then he'd always gotten off on the fact that she was wet for him on demand. What normal girl wouldn't be though?

Before she could voice some kind of acknowledgment, he tore the fragile material from her and discarded it to the floor. He tilted her chin up and commanded huskily, "Watch."

Her pussy clenched at the fierce possessiveness that shone in his stare reflecting back at her. His focus on her...all of her.

"See how perfect we look together?" he asked.

She nodded. She couldn't argue with that. At least, not until his hands cupped her breasts and he added, "We belong together, baby. Always."

# Chapter Two

**H**er breath hissed with denial, even as somewhere deep within, a seed of want burst into life.

"Don't say anything," he said when she opened her mouth to reject him outright, despite her inner yearnings, or perhaps because of them. "Not yet," he added gently, though there was steel in his gaze. "Just...think about it."

Her heart lurched. And for a moment, indecision nipped at all her hard-won years of self-assurance and inner poise with sharp little teeth.

Would becoming his mistress really be so bad?

*You know it would.*

Being exclusive to one man wouldn't make her any more important. In fact, aside from losing her other trusted clients, she'd also lose her independence. Her free will. And eventually, his interest.

Leaving her with nothing but a broken heart and shattered self-esteem. She was already an expert in the art of being abandoned by a loved one. And she really didn't know if she'd be strong enough the next time to pick up the pieces.

"I want you," he said, his expression intense, passionate. "You know I do. And I'll do anything to have you, if you'll let me."

She should have felt a little fear, a little trepidation. She didn't. Something thrilling took hold of her insides even before one of his hands dropped to her waist, the other taking hold of his shaft and guiding it forward.

With a harsh grunt, he thrust deep inside her. She cried out, needing this physical connection so bad it hurt. He stroked in and out with a steadily building, relentless rhythm as he added hoarsely, "We're perfect together."

She wasn't about to argue, not while a torrent of sensation was pulling her under and having its wicked way with her. She stared at the reflection of their joined bodies, unable to drag her eyes away.

Her pulse stuttered and soared at the vision of Blaine rocking behind her. She wanted only to drag out the moment, the undeniable thrill of just being with this man. With her breasts swinging and wisps of her hair tumbling free and causing her to look even more wanton than usual, it was a visual turn-on that was as close to decadent as the act itself.

The familiar wonder of an orgasm pressed at her senses. Overwhelming. And yet just out of reach.

Blaine's brilliant eyes held hers in the mirror as he parted the flesh of her labia with seeking, skillful hands, and deftly massaged the nub of her clit. She sucked in a breath. Then his name spilled from her lips and she shattered hard as pleasure ricocheted through her system, and then shot her to the heights and beyond.

Triumph flashed across Blaine's face a nanosecond before his head fell back, his jaw clenched tight as his seed pulsed deep.

She had no idea how long they stayed joined with her head slumped back on his chest, his hands cupping her pussy as if he didn't want to lose their intimate connection. But at some stage, Blaine disengaged from her wet heat and turned her around to lift her into his arms.

She tucked her head close to all his damp, male heat, inhaling the musky scent of his skin infused with the even muskier scent of sex.

With the music an accompanying throb to her still thundering pulse, he carried her up a flight of stairs and threw open a door. A side lamp cast a dull glow over the huge bedroom. Floor-to-ceiling windows revealed faraway views of the Sydney Harbor Bridge and Opera House illuminated by sparkling lights.

The new crimson comforter on his huge four-poster bed made her smile a little. She understood now his desire for her to wear red.

Though he wielded plenty of power in the boardroom and beyond, real passion appeared to be something he relished in his private time.

He laid her on the soft-as-a-cloud bed, his expression tender. "Brandy, I wanted to talk to you—"

The insistent chime of his cell phone claimed his attention. His face tightened, lips pressed into a line. Releasing a breath, he pressed a kiss to her brow and murmured, "I'd better answer. It must be important." He smiled. "Don't go anywhere, hmm?"

Before she could reply, he'd already swung away from her. She blinked. He'd been about to say something important, she was damn well certain of it. Whether it was something she actually wanted to hear, she might not ever find out now.

Switching the music off with a remote, he retrieved the cell from his bedside table. "Blaine Waymann," he said tersely.

Heading toward his bedroom balcony, he pushed open the sliding glass door and stepped outside. A cool breeze caressed her body and filtered his voice her way. "Sam, this'd better be goddamned important. When I said I didn't want any interruptions..."

Brandy frowned as his voice trailed off. She could only assume Sam was his PA, or someone who handled his day-to-day business dealings. But why didn't Blaine want to be disturbed? He was a renowned business shark, an entrepreneur and prolific money maker. Surely one night with her wasn't more important than the thrill of wheeling and dealing?

She wasn't sure how long she laid on his bed, mulling over the implications of her thoughts, before Blaine returned, his expression tense. He rubbed the back of his neck, then looked her way. His hand dropped and a smile curved his lips. "How did I ever believe I'd get you out of my system?" he murmured. He leaned over the bed, his mouth capturing hers in a gentle kiss.

Her breath caught in her throat and yearning stirred once again in her belly before he pulled back and informed her, "That was my secretary, calling to remind me about a charity fundraiser I'm attending Saturday night. I know it's short notice, but I'd love for you to come with me."

She frowned. He looked so serious, his eyes searching hers as though he wanted to decipher her every thought. She swallowed past a suddenly dry throat, aware something between them tonight had taken a major leap and there wasn't a damn thing she could do to stop it. "This Saturday?" At his nod she shook her head. She was booked two months in advance. Changing her schedule with two days to spare wasn't possible. "Sorry, I can't."

Something glinted in his eyes, something dark, dangerous. "Whatever your client is paying, I'll triple it."

She pushed herself up onto her elbows. She'd learned long ago not to back down on the important stuff, and this was monumentally important. This was her future. "It's not about the money."

He straightened, his face unreadable, though a flash of skepticism lit tellingly in his stare. Then he nodded, striding toward a walk-in closet before returning with a pile of his clothes in hand. He shrugged into a white business shirt. "Stay the night," he suggested softly. Yet his every word screamed a seriousness that underlined their mutual sexual relationship really had gone beyond the point of a business transaction. "Sleep here. I need to sort out some business merger issues. When I get back, we'll talk."

And finish what he'd been about to tell her before his cell phone conversation? She didn't argue, didn't agree either. In his mind, it was all settled. As a high-powered businessman, he was used to being obeyed. But something shriveled inside her, even as a great, aching sadness filled her, while she watched him dress.

He slung a tie around his throat and she stood, with practiced hands, slipping it behind his collar before knotting it just how he liked it. She should know. She'd had plenty of practice unknotting his ties.

He lifted a hand, the back of his knuckles brushing across her jaw. A lingering touch. "Thanks, Brandy...Kate."

He didn't seem to notice her shocked intake of breath. Didn't seem to realize his obvious investigating into her past was the final straw.

He retrieved his cell phone before he turned to her and gathered her stiff body to him for a brief, tender kiss. "Sweet dreams, baby. I'll be back as soon as I can."

*And you won't find me here.*

Hot tears spilled down her face as she listened to the muffled thud of his footsteps retreating downstairs and through the ground floor of his home. The front door slammed, followed soon after by the faint clunk of his car door. Then the Porsche's engine thrummed to life in the driveway.

Only when the sound of its motor had long dissolved into the distance did she swipe away her tears. She'd never slept a whole night in a client's bed—because that was all he was, a client—and she wasn't about to start now.

She was too professional to let business mix with her personal life.

Resolve steeled her spine as she made her way down the staircase and into the entertainment room. Blaine expected her to throw away her whole future on the off chance he'd want her as his mistress for longer than a few months. Because that was all it would take for their semi-permanent living arrangement to start to pall, surely?

Better to cut all ties now rather than later, when things could only get more complicated and messy.

The flames in the glass-domed fireplace had died down to little more than glowing embers when she retrieved her dress and slipped it back on, her fingers unsteady as she drew up the zipper.

She glanced at her ripped-beyond-repair thong. She'd have to do without it. No great feat for someone in her profession.

Retrieving her clutch purse and fishing inside it for her cell phone, she pressed speed dial to put a call through to her agency, requesting immediate pickup. Disconnecting, she took one last look around the room, trying not to think too hard about the glorious sex that had occurred here such a short time ago.

Trying hard not to think about the man she couldn't see anymore.

Breath shuddered from her lungs. Damn. How quickly things could change.

She dropped the cell back into her purse at about the same time she saw the square foil packages peeking out at her. She put a hand to her mouth. For the first time since she'd become a call girl, she hadn't given a thought to using a condom.

Her mouth pulled tight. Of course, being on the pill meant pregnancy was no cause for concern. But disease was always a risk, always a factor, no matter that she now only kept a handful of select clients.

*Fool*!

Her heart twisted, leaving a sick feeling in her belly. It was yet another reason she had to put a stop to seeing Blaine. No amount of money and amazing sex was worth sacrificing everything she'd worked so damn hard to build.

It really was time to leave. Permanently.

# Chapter Three

**K**ate sucked in deep breaths even as she increased her pace on the treadmill, enjoying the rush of adrenaline and fatigue. Sweat dribbled down her back and stuck her t-shirt to her torso and her tiny, lycra shorts to her butt.

"Wow, Kate. You're really working off some steam."

She turned to her friend and fellow VIP Agency call girl, and managed a smile. All the girls used their real names when out in public—they had to if they wanted to keep their occupations secret. Working names were reserved exclusively for clients. "You know me too well."

Claire Davis—Scarlet—pushed back a lock of her flame-red hair that had escaped its high ponytail, then smiled a secret smile as she stepped onto the treadmill next to Kate's. "So I should, after all our gym sessions and lunches with the girls."

Kate nodded. It was odd how her once so-called friendships at school had quickly petered out, while a handful of the VIP escorts had become her closest friends. It was like a secret club, where the seriousness of their profession was left behind with weekly lunches and the occasional shopping sprees.

Claire was the only other woman from the agency who loved the gym as much as Kate did. Kate had also recently discovered that Claire was the only other woman who'd fallen for a client. The gorgeous redhead constantly struggled not to crack under the pretense that she was fine.

It was yet another reason Kate was determined not to give into the desire to be with Blaine. Not just because it went against their agency's rules. A wealthy man and an escort might make a viable bedroom partnership short-term, but from what she'd seen, anything more just wasn't emotionally healthy or sustainable.

The situation between Claire and her once regular client, Mackenzie, was exacerbated by the fact that Kate had unwittingly taken him on as a regular. But Claire had insisted that Kate not cancel the arrangement she had with Mackenzie; insisted that business was business...as long as things never got personal.

Kate had relented. If she had crossed Mackenzie off her exclusive list, he would have found someone else. And in her and Claire's line of work, personal feelings had to be pulverized under a very sharp heel.

Claire began to do a slow, warm-up jog beside Kate, her stride effortless and graceful, and revealing a love of fitness and running. "Want to talk about it?"

Ignoring her screaming muscles, Kate managed to smile at the gorgeous woman in her cheetah-print sports top and a pair of black spandex leggings. Claire had the slender, toned body of an athlete, and turned heads wherever she went. Any man would be crazy not to return her feelings. "It's a...client."

If anyone could relate, it was Claire.

The redhead jerked her attention back to Kate, then asked sharply, "Who?"

Kate swiped a damp hand over her face, ignoring the sharp twist of hurt in her belly. "Don't worry, it's not Mackenzie."

Claire grimaced. "Sorry...I didn't mean...what I'm saying is...I know I can trust you."

A trust that was entirely limited to Kate and Mackenzie's intimacy being a purely professional transaction.

Kate withheld a sigh. "It's okay. I know you're not thinking straight right now."

Claire nodded. "Yeah, you've got that right." She jabbed a button on the treadmill and picked up the pace. "So what is it with your client?" Concern tightened her mouth and sharpened her tone. "He's not forcing you to do anything you don't want to, is he?"

Kate might have laughed if the subject matter wasn't so serious. "Not even close. In fact, he's a respectful and attentive lover."

"And?"

"And I'm worried he's starting to get too... attached."

More likely obsessed, but Claire didn't need to know all the details. It was just a relief to talk to someone else about it.

"Ah." The redhead sent her a considering look. "It happens. We're paid to be every man's fantasy. They only see us perfectly dressed and groomed, not to mention beyond willing to please them in the bedroom."

Kate tried not to let her emotions influence the stark truth. "Guess we're not the wives or girlfriends with tangled hair and bleary eyes from lack of sleep."

Claire snorted, sounding tired and jaded. "Oh, we might be childless, but we still get the bags under our eyes after a night servicing a man's every whim."

Kate turned to the other woman. Out of the handful of her call-girl friends, Claire was probably the most skilled at concealing her innermost emotions. Something was definitely up. "Enough about me. Are *you* okay?"

Claire sighed. "Sorry, I'm fine. I'm just having one of those days."

"You're still missing Mackenzie?" Kate asked softly.

Claire nodded. "Yeah, I really am." She swiped a piece of her bright-colored hair from her brow. "So...when is your next booking with Mackenzie?"

*Oh, shit.*

"Tonight."

Claire's already alabaster skin paled even further. But she managed to keep an even tone when she said softly, "He thinks I don't have feelings for him."

Kate almost lost her rhythm, and she slowed the machine to allow her heart rate and breathing to settle as she cooled down. "Why would he think that?"

The other woman shrugged. "Because that's what I told him." She turned shimmering green eyes Kate's way. "Because I didn't want him to know the truth and have him use it against me."

Kate left the gym with sweat still hovering on her brow and every muscle hurting. She'd never been one to do things by halves, but she'd pushed herself hard today, harder than ever before.

But like it or not, nothing could stop the constant thoughts about Blaine. She simply had to weather the storm until such time as his desire for her blew over. Her belly cramped at the thought of him giving up on her, or worse, finding someone else just like Mackenzie had with Claire.

No, she had to instead focus on everyday tasks, like keeping herself in tip-top shape. Stamina and an amazing body were prerequisites if she wanted to continue in the escort business. And then, when the time came for her to leave, she'd retire a wealthy, fit and still-young woman with money invested in various nest eggs. She'd be self-sufficient for the rest of her years.

By then, whatever connection she and Blaine had developed, would be long forgotten...a distant memory.

*Yeah, right.*

She'd half expected him to show up at her apartment that morning, not that she'd ever told him the address. But since he'd learned her name, it stood to reason he would also know where she lived. She frowned. As a call girl, her privacy was nonnegotiable, to be guarded at all costs.

All her clients knew and respected it.

Until now.

So why had something inside her shriveled a little when Blaine hadn't shown? When he hadn't even rung the agency to leave her a message?

Hell, he probably had her cell phone number anyway. He would have rung her direct.

She started when her cell phone abruptly chimed. Fishing through her gym bag, she dug it out. Disappointment bit deep at seeing the ID on her cell. Maisey, the woman who ran the VIP Agency with an iron fist.

"Brandy," she answered, deliberately going into character and cycling her real name to the back of her mind.

Maisey's voice cut straight to the chase. "You've had a cancellation."

Her shock was less at Maisey's faintly accusatory tone and a whole lot more by the fact that someone had cancelled. She was booked solid for months in advance and had never once had someone rescind on their "date."

"Who?" she asked carefully, sounding normal in every way, if only she wasn't shrinking inside until she was again that little girl no one loved.

"Smitherson."

Mackenzie Smitherson. Her too-familiar feelings of inadequacy were quickly superseded by relief. A smile curled her lips. With any luck, her client had come to his senses in regards to Claire...Scarlet. Brandy's smile faltered. Maybe that would be a bad thing? Escorts were paid sex workers. Relationships weren't part of the package, and Scarlet stood to be hurt even more if things dragged out.

She cleared her throat. "He's booked for tonight. Is he sick?"

Maisey huffed out a breath. "Sounded pissed as hell, but healthy as a horse."

*What the hell?*

"Has he booked with one of the other girls?" she asked cautiously.

She had to be careful. Maisey was a bulldog when it came to privacy. The older woman was all too gifted at vocally flaying the girls if any one of them stepped out of line. But despite the cancellation, Maisey seemed relatively calm.

"No, you haven't lost your regular. Not yet, anyway."

She blew out a slow breath. Aside from Blaine, Mackenzie was fast becoming her best customer. A regular client who treated her well and paid even better. He was another powerful businessman and client who was quite the catch, as Scarlet had discovered to her detriment.

But Scarlet's predicament was precisely the road Brandy was heading down with Blaine. A path she had to exit sooner rather than later.

She nodded absently. At least she'd be alone tonight to lick her wounds. And quietly yearn for Blaine.

"Never mind though," Maisey added into the silence, her voice clearly appeased, "I've managed to rebook you with another regular."

Her heart sank. "Actually, I'd prefer not to—"

Maisey's voice turned cajoling. "It's triple the going rate."

She should have known. Blaine. It had to be. Odd the quickening of her pulse, the pull of her belly and the shortness of her breath that had zilch to do with her exercise regime and all to do with her pathetic needs. She cleared her throat once again, needing verification. "Who?"

"Waymann." Maisey said his name meaningfully and Brandy heard something in the other woman's tone that hinted she could do far worse.

Well, duh. If she wasn't in the escort business, she would have slept with Blaine for free—not that she'd have met him anyway, unless she'd somehow managed to claw her way up into the high social echelons he kept.

Silence breached the conversation for a moment as Brandy sifted through her thoughts and temptation suckered her in. Tonight could be her final hurrah, the grand finale before she said goodbye to him one last time.

She took a deep breath. "Okay."

"I knew you'd come to your senses. He'll be expecting you. Six p.m. sharp," Maisey said, voice brisk and business-like again. "I'll send you the car. Oh, and one more thing. He said dress casual."

As opposed to wearing a slutty outfit suited to a night of whoring in his bed?

As the connection abruptly cut, Kate clutched the cell as if it was a lifeline. It wasn't. An odd sense of knowing came over her. Blaine had orchestrated the whole thing, had paid Mackenzie off, or more likely, called in a favor to have her all to himself.

A surge of irrational pleasure was thrust aside to make way for an unhealthy dose of resentment.

*Fuck.*

Her whole career could be at stake, thanks to Blaine's obsessive nature.

It appeared he'd really meant it when he'd told her she'd pay.

She tossed her cell phone back into her bag before she lifted her chin and walked the ten minutes to her chic, inner-city apartment. If Blaine wanted her that badly tonight, then so be it.

But this would definitely be their last time together.

# Chapter Four

**B**laine stood on the balcony of his townhouse, a brandy snifter in hand, while he gazed out over the darkening sky of the city. Twilight was settling over Sydney.

This time of day usually relaxed him. Even after hours in the office, he took the time to appreciate the changing of day to night. But this time he was restless, and all but blind to the picturesque sundown unfolding before his eyes.

Not even business matters could distract him from the woman who'd gotten under his skin and lodged deep in his heart. His every thought was consumed by her; even asleep, he dreamed about her.

He took a deep slug of his drink. Only a few nights ago, he'd dreamed that Kate—she'd always be Kate to him now, not Brandy—had walked toward him in a wedding gown. She'd looked radiant in a white lace creation and wispy veil, with her strawberry-blonde hair drifting over one shoulder and a bouquet of crimson roses in hand.

She might be far from being a virgin, but the virtuousness of the wedding dress had looked perfect on her. No doubt because she was as pure of heart as any woman he'd ever met, a beautiful seductress who glowed with inner goodness.

A man could all too easily lose himself to her. Hell, he'd lost himself to her from the very first moment he'd seen Brandy at a function with another client. Until that moment, he'd never believed in fairytales, or even true love. That she was a call girl hadn't ever bothered him. He grimaced. Jesus, he'd be beyond hypocritical to use the services of an escort agency and then hold any of the girls in contempt.

Not that he needed an escort to get laid. Women had always come onto him, and he'd never felt the need to go slow in a relationship, until Kate. He might be paying for her services, but he'd been courting her in every way except in the bedroom.

He swallowed the last of his brandy, barely tasting the burn going down his throat.

Sex with her might be uninhibited, out-and-out pleasure, but he'd handled every other aspect of their relationship with kid gloves. He had to if he had any chance with her long term.

Though call girls, by virtue of their profession, said little about themselves, he recognized in Kate a fear of true intimacy and trust. He sighed. Her issues probably hadn't been helped by their first tryst.

He only wished now he'd been more romantic, their date not just about the sex. But at the time, he'd been consumed by her, and totally thinking with the wrong head. He'd craved her like he was addicted and had been foolish enough to presume sating himself with her would get her out of his system.

He barked out a self-deprecating laugh, even as his mind drifted to that first fateful booking.

Blaine paced up and down the thick, gray carpet of the luxury penthouse he'd booked for the night. Damn it, he never paced! Then again, he'd never wanted another woman as badly as he did the blonde bombshell he'd paid top dollar for a night in his bed.

Not that the money mattered to him. He had more than enough to throw around. Hell, he'd have paid ten times that amount, from the moment he'd seen her at a charity function with a well-known senator who should have been more discreet.

But the senator seemed to thrive on a little scandal—it'd been said he had outstanding taste in women. Blaine had agreed wholeheartedly, until the man had married a dowdy woman with more money and social connections than sense.

Blaine stilled, his hands clenching. He could no more imagine the senator fucking his prim and uptight wife than he could the sexalicious Brandy. In fact, he didn't even want to think about the senator touching the same gorgeous call girl he also waited impatiently to touch, to kiss and to fuck.

It was frankly alarming that a woman he'd yet to officially meet could ignite such irrational jealousy. It was an emotion unfamiliar to him, and one he wouldn't endure any longer. But he was a man of control, just the same as he was a man of action. And it would be the latter he fed tonight, control be damned!

A knock sounded on the door. His cock jerked and his belly clenched into a knot of anticipation. His control already at the razor's edge, he strode toward the thick, mahogany door and dragged it open.

His breath caught in his throat. For the first time since...forever, he was at a loss for words. If from a distance, Brandy had been gorgeous, then up close and personal she was stunning.

Unlike the handful of paid escorts he'd been with in the past, Brandy was a breath of fresh air. Beautiful, sexy and classy in a flowing white gown with a tight-fitted, red bodice that gave a startling splash of color.

His mouth dried. He had a feeling he'd always associate this gorgeous woman with red. With passion, daring and power.

Even in stilettos, she had to crane her neck a little to look up and meet his gaze. Her eyes widened at his undoubtedly ravenous stare, her pearly white teeth grappling with her bottom lip. Then she smiled, blinking long, dark lashes that framed bright emerald eyes. A siren's stare. "You're expecting me," she said huskily.

The sound of her voice had his cock stretching to impossible dimensions, his balls heavy and aching for release. He didn't bother with small talk, instead he nodded and held out his hand. She reached out slender fingers and he drew her inside and kicked the door shut.

Her eyes widened again, even before he pushed her up against the solid wood and plundered her sexy mouth, his fingers ransacking her upswept hair. Jesus, was kissing allowed? Was it against the agency's code? But his thoughts no sooner formed before they dissolved, his whole being focused on nothing more than taking Brandy...possessing her.

Her clutch purse dropped to the carpet with a muffled thud, and then she was kissing him back with an urgent little moan. Holy shit, she really knew how to kiss. But he'd bet Brandy had spent many years perfecting the art of seduction; of how to please a man.

Lip contact clearly wasn't against the VIP Agency's rulebook.

His cock strained behind his pants, and he pushed his tongue between her lips before kicking his legs apart to grind his erection between her thighs. His hands tightened on her scalp. Was she happy being with men for money? Was it her decision or did she feel she had no choice? Or was being every man's fantasy her true calling?

Why it mattered to him barely registered, all he knew was that it did. It mattered a lot. But there'd be plenty of time to find out everything about Brandy. Right now, he was enough of a bastard to forget everything and cede to his passion; to the woman whose legs wrapped around his hips as she moaned into his mouth. Right now, all of the hundred and one questions in his head were fast becoming background noise as lust surged to the fore.

His kiss deepened and he sucked in her honeyed breath. It didn't mean he couldn't show *her* what it was to be pleasured. He'd make sure that this time she too would be at the receiving end of glorious satisfaction.

He pulled back from her, his whole body vibrating with barely withheld lust as he said succinctly, "I'm going to take you right here, right now, against the door. And I'm not going to be gentle."

Her eyes flared in shock, and then slowly turned slumberous with heat. She nodded and said huskily, "Condoms are in my purse."

His cell rang, jerking him back to the present with a start. He squeezed his eyes shut, for a moment ignoring the jarring sound as he waited until the powerful memories slipped quietly into the back of his mind. Then, dragging the phone out of his pocket, he checked caller ID before he answered.

The real estate agent wasn't someone he wanted to ignore right now. Not when he wanted to finalize all the last, nit-picky details on his latest and most important piece of real estate.

Then he could focus tonight on Kate.

He no sooner disconnected when his cell buzzed through with another call, demanding his attention. This time he couldn't help but smile on seeing the caller ID. "Hello, Mother."

"Blaine, I'm glad I finally managed to catch you."

His smile widened. His mother liked to harp on about how little time he left himself for socializing, which included family phone calls. "I'm glad too."

Her delicate sigh told him she was slightly appeased. "I just wanted to check you hadn't up and disappeared out of the country again."

His mouth almost hurt from the grin pulling at his lips. "Actually, being away from home no longer has any appeal. And before you ask, I *am* planning on visiting you very soon."

"See that you do. Now...why the sudden desire to stay in Sydney?" Her tone pitched higher. "Wait. Is there a special someone I should know about?"

He wondered if his mother had heard through the grapevine about the woman he'd been seeing quite a lot lately. If she had, then she'd clearly yet to discover that the same certain someone special he'd been seeing was also seeing other men.

His heart twisted in his chest, his hand tightening on his cell. Kate's chosen profession might not bother him in some ways, but knowing she was sleeping with other men was doing in his head. Sharing her was simply no longer an option.

He just had to convince Kate that *he* was all she'd ever need.

"So it *is* true!" his mother squawked with unfettered delight.

Damn. He'd asked for that. Being lost in thought and too slow to respond hadn't worked in his favor.

He pulled in a steadying breath. In all honesty, he wanted to proclaim to the world about the woman he loved. But that didn't mean Kate was of the same mindset, for obvious reasons. She was a call girl, being intensely private was par for the course.

"Well?" his mother demanded.

"There...is someone I like," he conceded carefully. He had to play this safe. The last thing he or Kate needed was for his mother to go and pry into his personal life to dig up all the facts.

"Oh, wonderful news!" his mother said gaily into his ear. "When are you seeing her next?"

He braced himself for the inescapable invite even as he said slowly, "Actually, I'm taking her out to dinner tonight." And then to bed. He was planning a night of multiple orgasms for them both.

Good thing his mother couldn't read his mind.

"Then bring her here first. Please Blaine," she cajoled, "you know I'm not getting any younger."

If there was any woman who could manipulate him at all, it was his mother. Then again, few women could say they'd taken on a business single-handedly after their so called bread-winning husband had died.

Not only had his mother taken on the fabric printing company, she'd turned it into a success. A miracle, being that the company had been on the brink of bankruptcy and she'd had no prior knowledge or experience of how to run it.

She'd learned the whole process herself, had been thrown into the deep end without a life preserver in sight. All that, and she'd been a single mother raising a boy on the threshold of becoming a teen. A young man with unresolved anger issues, but a deep and abiding love for his mother.

In the end, he was only glad he'd taken after his mother and not his good-for-nothing father who'd died of a heart attack while boozing, snorting coke and womanizing with a trio of whores.

He absently scrubbed a hand along his brow. Evidently it was his dad's side that Blaine took after when it came to paid sex.

He grimaced, and then said carefully into the phone, "You really make it hard to refuse."

"You know I'll love her."

"I'm certain you will."

Brandy's occupation not so much.

Although his mother was a mix of modern and old school—she'd been raised by stout Catholics and yet was open-minded in many ways—he was certain the pain and humiliation left behind by a cheating husband hadn't diminished.

"Wonderful! I'll expect you both for a couple of pre-dinner drinks."

He arched a brow at her glee, staring unseeingly at the lights blinking into the darkness as he ended the call with, "Sounds good. We'll see you then."

He disconnected the call, then pressed speed dial to connect him to the VIP Agency. He had another booking to make for tomorrow night with Brandy, and he'd pay whatever necessary to make it happen.

# Chapter Five

**B**randy dragged her feigned interest away from the passing shadowy bush-land outside the passenger window of Blaine's sedan. Ignoring the fluttering in her belly, she smoothed away an imaginary crease in her lacy crimson bustier and skirt, before turning to face her client.

She withheld a sigh at Blaine's brooding silence. No other man made her feel so cherished and self-assured; yet left her so unsettled, as though her whole world irrevocably changed with every second spent in his company.

Knowing tonight would be over sooner rather than later left her even more out of kilter. She wanted this date to end even as she wanted to cherish their remaining time together. He might be obsessed with her, but what if she too was steering that same direction for him?

Not. Going. To. Happen.

She put a hand on his thigh, stroking up and down his jeans leg and causing his muscle to contract beneath.

Whatever her feelings, it was unprofessional not to give Blaine exactly what he'd paid her for. As a high-class escort, she was exceptionally good at her job, and she'd do well to remember it. A pity her interest in him seemed lately to be less about business and more personal.

But no matter her chaotic emotions, she had to focus on her client. She'd never seen him so quiet and restrained. "Blaine, is something wrong?"

It wasn't often that a visit to his house resulted in going out for dinner first and sex later. And though he'd been his usual gallant self, something clearly weighed on his mind.

Was he pissed about coming home to an empty house on their last date? He should have been grateful. Sex with her was costing him a small fortune, but leaving her to sleep alone a whole night in his bed would be a luxury few men would consider. Not that Blaine seemed to care about the steep escort rates.

The shiver that went all the way to her toes was less fear and more unwitting excitement. Lately, he didn't seem to care about anything but having her exclusively to himself.

He glanced at her with a smile, the dash lights somehow picking up the gold glints in his eyes. "Sorry, I was deep in thought." His smile turned rueful. "Not particularly the memorable date I'd intended."

"Every date with you is memorable," she said huskily. It might sound like a practiced speech she gave all her clients, but it was scarily true. For someone in her line of work who lived for sex, it was crazy-town to love every single minute; every sexual encounter with one man.

Maybe because, although Blaine was unfailingly a gentleman, he was anything *but* one in the bedroom. There, he was a master player, a virtuoso, a man who knew exactly how to please a woman. A man who knew when to take her rough and fast, and when to give it to her infinitely slow and tender.

He could easily have been in the escort industry himself, leaving in his wake dozens of satisfied women too weak to drag up their cum-soaked panties. She smiled at the thought, even as something twisted a little inside.

Not that she was remotely jealous. That one word was reviled in her profession. She just had to remember this date was nothing more than business. And though she might have been peeved about him changing up her schedule, and possibly creating waves with Mackenzie, right now it felt all too right being with Blaine.

"You don't pay me to have to always put on the charm." She needed to remind them both of why she was here with him. She turned to him and shrugged. "You've had a rough day. I totally get it."

She slid her hand a little higher, lingering at the top of his thigh. "Why don't I help you forget whatever's troubling you?"

He dragged in a ragged breath and flicked on the indicator before turning off the motorway that'd taken them North of Sydney. "Baby, you're playing with fire."

She idly traced the bulging outline of his arousal, enjoying every hard inch of him imprisoned beneath his jeans. Almost as much as she enjoyed his ragged breaths and clenched hands. Scraping a tapered fingernail along the swollen contours of his cock, she said hoarsely, "Maybe I want to be your gasoline."

He groaned out an expletive and pulled the car off the road, where a couple of spreading gum trees sheltered a stretch of grass. Parking behind the nearest tree, with what appeared to be distant rolling hills as their backdrop, he turned glowing eyes her way. "I want you. Right here. Right now."

Her mouth dried and her senses heightened. This was the mood she always wanted Blaine to be in with her. Aroused. Stimulated. Desperate to have her!

She unclipped her seatbelt with unsteady hands. Hitching up her skirt and about to drag down her lacy thong, he growled, "I'll push them aside."

*Holy fuck.* His harsh urgency had her womb clench and her pussy moisten in anticipation. Then again, everything about Blaine was thrilling and exciting.

She climbed onto him, straddling him even as he unzipped and unbuttoned his jeans. She helped push them down along with his boxer briefs far enough to free the big, hard length of him.

Her belly contracted. How was such a gorgeous specimen of a male also lucky enough to be gifted with the perfect weapon? She might not be able to see much more than shadows in the gloom, but she knew his cock intimately. It would be engorged and ribbed with veins, the slit undoubtedly beading with pre-cum.

Her mouth watered at the thought of tasting him, drawing in his salty essence before sucking his hard, pulsating length into her mouth.

She fisted his shaft instead, and was rewarded by his shuddering breath that morphed into a growl as she moved her hand up and down. She'd never get enough of turning this man on, never get enough of his cock. It was mouth-watering, silky-smooth velvet encasing unyielding steel.

"You're killing me," he said hoarsely.

She smiled. His words were the sweetest music to her ears. When she moved off him to grab a condom from her purse, he clamped big hands around her waist and rasped, "You're not going anywhere."

Though she recognized the alpha male in him; rejoiced in it even, her smile evaporated. However much she might want to grind herself on his bare cock and relieve a little of the ache within, safe sex was paramount.

She refused to acknowledge the fact they'd already slipped up once in that regard. "We need to use protection."

His eyes burned in the shadows that were barely chased away by a quarter moon sitting high in the heavens. "I'm safe, and I know you are."

She gasped. "You had someone look into my medical records?"

His jaw clenched. "You want me to pretend I didn't? I'm no Boy Scout, you know that."

She didn't have the strength of will right now to argue. In anyone's eyes, what he'd done had been wrong. But then, he'd probably done plenty of wrong in the past to get to where he was in the corporate world. He was clearly a man willing to fight dirty for what or who he wanted.

Damn it all to hell if that didn't turn her on all the more!

His stare holding hers, he rubbed his thumb along her damp thong, intensifying her needs until she was moaning and writhing against him, and every one of her good intentions dissolved like mist in the desert.

With an aroused and self-satisfied smile, he dragged the lacy material of her thong to one side. Lifting his hips, he clamped hold of his shaft and rubbed its head over her clit.

Her breath hissed as electricity sizzled through her nerve endings. "Fuck. You. Blaine," she moaned.

He wasn't playing fair and he knew it. It didn't stop his smirk, didn't stop the repressed need darkening his face. "I believe that's exactly what we're doing."

She closed her eyes and threw her head back, clutching at his shoulders as he stimulated her sex so thoroughly, she was all too quickly climbing toward a toe-curling climax that would soon leave her convulsing with pleasure.

He dragged down her bustier with his free hand, exposing her breasts. At the wet, warm pull of his mouth on her flesh, she whimpered, way past caring about anything but having him inside her.

He suckled, licked and nipped each breast, even as he continued to rhythmically press the head of his cock around her vulva. Alternating between soft and hard, fast and slow, and then easing back just seconds before she shuddered with relief.

The bastard knew exactly what he was doing. In fact, she might just die from repressed orgasm...or too much pleasure. Maybe both.

Releasing her breast, he whispered into her ear, "I'm going to keep hold of my cock, and you're going to impale yourself on me."

Her breath hissed. She was all but rabid with desire. Beyond caring about anything but pleasure. Beyond the ability to even recall the need for a condom.

Her hands digging into his shoulders, she watched him watching her as she slid ever so slowly down his thick length, her inner muscles greedily clasping his thickness. She had no doubt she shared his dazed expression, and as he sucked in a taut breath, she knew there was nothing better than this oneness with Blaine.

She pressed her lips over his, stealing his breath even while she began to rock up and down, slowly at first, and then with ever-increasing speed. He groaned, his lashes fluttering and his eyes gleaming. She let go of his mouth and pushed her hips forward, grinding her clit against the veined ridges of his cock until everything within her quivered and her dew caused a wet slap with every downward motion.

Blaine grabbed her hips and met her every thrust. She gasped at the intense friction that forced an orgasm to barrel through her like a freight train. As her inner muscles clenched around him, he growled out her name, and in the dim light, his eyes glazed over and his warm seed erupted inside her.

She was still dragging in deep breaths when she leaned her brow against his, staring down into his brilliant eyes. He lifted a hand, tracing her jaw. "You're amazing."

"You're not so bad yourself," she said softly.

He kissed her, slow and tenderly, and with more emotion than she'd ever experienced from him before. It made her realize how things were quickly getting too complex, too scarily real.

Because 'real' was yet another word not allowed in her world. Fantasy and make-believe was all it'd ever be.

She pulled back and his eyes darkened before he reluctantly released her. Scrambling back into the passenger seat, she adjusted her thong and pushed her skirt back into place.

She didn't want to know what Blaine was thinking or feeling, though she felt his stare on her long seconds before he leaned over and clipped her seatbelt into place. She repressed a wry smile. He cared about her safety, yet he'd fucked her without protection.

Then again, he would have been one hundred percent sure of them both being clean and her on the pill before he'd put anyone at risk.

He was nothing if not prepared.

As he took to the road once again, she did her best to re-pin her 'just fucked' hair into some semblance of a topknot, before reapplying a smear of crimson lipstick. She had no idea where they were going, but Blaine paid good money for her to look her best, and she wouldn't disappoint.

She turned to face him, approving the way his white dress shirt contrasted with his inky black hair and golden skin. Admiring even more how their lovemaking had somehow only enhanced his appeal. "Should I ask now where you're taking me?"

He cocked a brow. "Dinner at a lovely Italian restaurant. But not before you meet someone."

She frowned. That was highly irregular. A function or large gathering meant she could be friendly while maintaining a professional distance. But someone singular implied an affection or closeness to Blaine that didn't sit right with her. "Oh?"

"I think you'll like her."

Brandy's mind whirled. "Her?"

He nodded. "My mother."

What. The. Actual. Fuck. He was making things *way* too personal. "That's not a good idea."

His hands tightened on the steering wheel when he asked, "You accept money for sex. How bad can it be to get paid to socialize?"

Her face heated even as hurt bit deep. It wasn't what she'd meant and he damn well knew it. He was crossing a line in the sand by introducing her to a family member. "You know my skill at socializing is second to none," she said stiffly. She had to be poised when clients mixed business with pleasure. "What I'm *not* so skilled at is meeting a client's family and giving them the mistaken impression I'm a girlfriend."

"Who says it's mistaken?" he asked savagely. When she turned to him with wide eyes, he scraped a hand through his hair and said wearily,

"We both know that what we have between us is more than call girl and client."

Exactly the reason she wouldn't be seeing him again after tonight. But she wasn't going to tell him that right now. Not with things getting so serious. She'd survived in the industry by using her wits and trusting her instincts. She'd go along with his wishes for now. It didn't mean she'd give him false hope. "You're not the first client to think that way," she said gently.

"Maybe not," he grated. "But I'm betting I'm the first client you've returned feelings for."

She turned away, her heart rate flailing even as he exhaled with harsh satisfaction.

She'd be the first to admit her self-assurance sky-rocketed knowing men paid for the privilege of her company. But she'd never expected to develop feelings for a man, or worse, for a man to become so obsessed with her. But she had to put a stop to this...illusion between them before it escalated.

She turned to him and asked silkily, "Does your mother know I'm a whore?"

He flinched. "Is that how you want her to see you?"

"No matter how much you try and pretty it up, I screw men for money."

His breath hissed. "You also have a beautiful pussy that I love to lick and fuck. But I'm never going to call it a cunt." He looked at her, really looked. "I wouldn't belittle you like that."

She swallowed hard. He wasn't going to give her up without a fight, and right now, she had no idea how she was going to break the news to him that she intended to end their arrangement, once and for all, how she should have already terminated things between them before they'd gotten this far.

He indicated a few minutes later. Turning onto another road, his car headlights revealed what appeared to be a new housing estate. He glanced her way. "It's completely up to you if you want to tell my mother about your occupation."

"And you'd be okay with that?"

It wasn't dark enough to hide his frown. "You know I'm not ashamed of who you are."

And yet it was obvious something actually *did* bother him about her career choice. She sighed. She shouldn't feel so deflated. Ninety-nine percent of the population would probably be bothered by it.

She turned to him. "It doesn't really matter what I think. What I *know* is that your mother wouldn't care to hear that her son wants to be with me. At least, not once she uncovers the real me."

He slowed the car and sent her a long look. She let loose with a weary sigh. "I am what I am. I'm not going to go out of my way to change someone's opinion of me."

He looked ahead, his jaw tight and his voice flat. "You love your work that much?"

She blinked. "Yeah. I do." How could she not love financial independence and security? Not to mention physical stimulation and satisfaction with clients she knew and trusted. But even as she affirmed it out loud, she wondered privately if the gloss had started to wear off just a little.

"Kate, I..."

"I'm not Kate," she said sharply. "Brandy is my working name, and right now I *am* working. You're my client. Nothing more."

The glow of dash lights showed a muscle in his jaw flicker. "Of course I am. Thank you for the reminder."

# Chapter Six

**B**randy had worked through many difficult times as an escort, and yet she was left feeling undone by the taut silence filling the sedan as Blaine pulled into the red-paved driveway of a brick home with a gorgeously manicured lawn.

He cut the engine and headlights. About to open his door and climb out, she put a hand on his arm. "Blaine, I don't want us to fight..."

"Let's just get through the next half hour with some level of graciousness, hmm."

She blinked, startled by his terseness. *Shit.* She'd allowed her personal feelings to intrude on the job. Blaine was supposed to be enjoying himself, not regretting the decision to spend good money to be with her.

*Perhaps it's for the best*, a little voice interjected.

She lifted her chin. She'd never left a client dissatisfied, and she wasn't about to start now. Especially not with the one man who treated her more like a princess than a paid escort.

Blaine opened the passenger door and she accepted his proffered hand before climbing out. She smiled weakly. Even when he was displeased with her, he was still a gentleman, still a man worth his weight in gold.

It wasn't until they stood at his mother's front door that trepidation began to fill her from the inside out. If this woman was even half as smart as her son, she'd perceive something wasn't right between them.

Blaine pressed the doorbell, and the door swung open to an elegant woman dressed in a white shift dress, her short-styled dark hair running to gray. She smiled at them, exuding warmth even as she scolded Blaine.

"You know you don't have to knock on my door." She stepped toward him to claim a hug, before withdrawing to take a good look at Brandy. "And who is this gorgeous girl?"

Blaine turned to her, and Brandy froze with sudden indecision. There was a reason that call girls never met family members. She felt like a deer caught in headlights. Then she released a taut breath, smiled and said, "I'm...Kate."

The older woman returned her smile. "Kate, I'm Elaine. It's lovely to finally meet you."

So Elaine had heard about her then? She had doubts that Blaine would have brought her name up in a conversation, for obvious reasons. But it was easy enough for the paparazzi, or even acquaintances, to notice whether Blaine had the same woman on his arm at different functions.

Giving herself no more time to second-guess everything, she dipped her head and said, "Lovely to meet you, too."

Elaine stepped aside and swept out a pale hand. "Please, come in."

The house was lovely. White walls mixed with bright splashes of color in cushions, throws and furnishings. Minimalist yet far from boring. But it was the photos on the walls that Kate tried her best not to show interest in.

Particularly the black-and-white photo of Blaine as a young boy—she could see it was him because of his intense, bright eyes—and the man standing beside him, who had to be his father. There were too many physical similarities.

Even as a rather scrawny eleven or twelve year-old boy, Blaine was growing into a man who'd soon turn heads. He held up a decent-sized fish in one hand, and a fishing rod in the other. And though he exuded pride from his catch, she could see the small gap between him and his father might as well have been a hundred-foot chasm.

"I hope you like wine?" Elaine asked as she retrieved glasses from an overhead cupboard in the kitchen.

Kate dragged her attention back to the other woman. She nodded, already feeling at ease. "Wine would be lovely."

"Great." Elaine poured them all a glass. "My son is more of a whiskey kind of man, but he tolerates my love of wine on his rare visits."

"Actually, I'm more of a brandy kind of man these days," he said smoothly.

Kate kept a straight face, but she wondered if her expression slipped when Elaine asked, "So tell me about yourself, Kate? What do you do for a living?"

Kate felt heat rush to her face before Blaine put his arm around her waist. "Mom please, grilling her already?"

Elaine had the grace to look sheepish. "Is it my fault I'm fascinated by the first woman my son has taken any real interest in?"

Kate pinned a smile in place even as her heart sank. So much for feeling at ease. Already the topic of conversation was getting personal. She gulped down a mouthful of wine, then cleared her throat and said, "You have a lovely home."

The other woman tactfully took the hint. "Thank you, dear. I retired a few years ago and decided I wanted to take things easy and live in a comfortable and easily maintained home."

"Mom lives alone," Blaine added. "Has been single, in fact, ever since my dad passed away when I was twelve."

A twinge of sympathy overshadowed Kate's discomfort. If anyone could relate to loss, she could. It couldn't have been easy for them to lose a husband; a father. Even a man as distant as the one she'd seen in the photo.

That snapshot might well have been the last taken of Blaine and his father together.

But at least Blaine had some memories of his father, hopefully ones that weren't all bad. Unlike the recollections she had of her own dear old dad. As a matter of fact, she wished a whole lot of her 'family' memories could be erased.

It was her father who'd instilled in her a conviction that men only liked women for their looks. Kate's mother had learned that they hard way.

Elaine nodded, dragging Kate back to the present as she said, "I'd like to say it's because Blaine's father was the love of my life, but I'd be lying." For a moment her face lost its warmth. "When I took over my husband's business, I was kept far too busy to worry about men."

Kate nodded, while inside, her belly dropped. Her life couldn't be more different from Elaine's. As an escort, her whole business *was* men.

Elaine swept a hand toward Blaine. "It was Blaine who kept me going when things got tough and overwhelming, with all my energy going into being the sole bread winner."

Kate had no doubt the other woman would hate her all the more, knowing her one and only son had feelings for a hooker. Still, she managed a semblance of a smile and said, "It's easy to see Blaine takes after you in everything business."

"Oh please, if only I *was* half as prolific and successful as my son." Elaine laughed as she topped up their glasses. "Still, I can't complain. I'm retired now and more than content." She gave her son a meaningful look. "Of course, if Blaine chose to give me some grandchildren in the not so distant future, I'd be a very happy woman."

Kate sucked in a shocked breath, even as Blaine said wryly, "Careful you don't scare my date away."

Elaine took a sip of her wine, her shrewd eyes landing on Kate. "So you're a career girl, then?"

Kate nodded. "I am."

A faint frown crossed Elaine's face, as though she wanted to know more but decided to bide her time. She turned back to Blaine, her head tilting to the side. "You know gossip travels fast."

Kate inhaled sharply even as the room began to slowly revolve. This was it then, the moment of truth. Despite Elaine's genuine warmth, she braced herself for the inevitable slurs. The questioning of her character and morals.

Blaine appeared indifferent, though his clasp on her tightened as if in reassurance. "Oh?"

Elaine nodded. "Whenever you're in Sydney, you get with the same gorgeous woman with strawberry-blonde hair. I *know* things must be getting serious with Kate."

Kate released the breath she'd held. *Holy shit.* Talk about being let off the hook. She'd expected harsh criticism, but instead got hopeful optimism that she and Blaine were getting together.

Blaine nodded. "Then I guess some rumors really aren't rumors." He turned to her. "I just have to convince Kate that what we have is real."

Kate mustered a smile, even as inwardly she wanted to stomp on Blaine's toes. He'd deliberately put her in the thick of things, put all the attention back on her.

Elaine's eyes turned speculative as they brushed over Kate. She was probably wondering who the hell wouldn't love her son. He was beyond handsome and successful. And Kate had no doubt he'd be faithful to the woman he loved.

But surely the novelty of living full time with one woman would wear thin on a man?

She took a deep swallow of the wine, aware its effects on an empty belly probably weren't doing her any favors. But at least if she was drinking she didn't have to talk. She had nothing to say in her defense.

A clock somewhere nearby loudly ticked away the seconds when Blaine murmured, "I might show Kate around."

His mother nodded. "Of course."

Kate was grateful for Blaine's arm around her as he led her through the lounge room and down a hallway. They stepped out onto a balcony, where late spring lent a balmy feel to the air.

She gazed up at the Milky Way, though it was Blaine's presence she was lost in.

"I apologize for the grilling," he said. "My mom might have a beautiful soul, but she also has the protective instincts of a pit-bull."

She drank the last of her wine and Blaine took it from her, placing the empty glass on a wooden table. He grinned. "Careful. I don't doubt for a second she's also doing her best to loosen your tongue."

Kate bit into her bottom lip. He was trying to lighten the mood, but her anxiety only intensified. She turned to him fully, catching the vague glint of his eyes in the dark. "I think we should tell your mom we're not a real couple."

His good mood vanished. "Are you *that* determined to ensure everyone knows we're not in a relationship?" he grated out.

"Blaine, I'm not your everyday girl next door. I'm not girlfriend material."

"I beg to differ."

She looked back out into the velvet darkness, where stars and houselights shone like beacons in the night. "You only see me as the sexy woman ready and willing to pleasure you. Normal life is rarely like that."

His sigh sounded loud in the thick silence of the night, broken only by the sporadic and far-off yapping of a dog. "Don't you get it? I'd give my right arm to see you in a flannelette nightgown and in my bed. Give anything to kiss you good-bye every morning, leaving you with your hair all mussed from a night in my arms."

She shoved aside the mental picture she badly wanted to make come true. But she wasn't prepared to become one man's mistress, not even for Blaine. "That's never going to happen." She turned to him, willing him to understand what she was about to tell him. "Blaine, we can't see each other anymore. You've paid to be with me tonight. But that's it. I'm telling the escort agency I can't see you anymore."

She didn't need to see his face to sense his utter shock. It was a pity she didn't also sense they weren't alone.

"Blaine...?"

Kate swallowed back a gasp at Elaine's shocked voice behind her. She twisted slowly, dreading how the interior lights would force her to witness Elaine's ashen face.

*Fuck.*

Elaine wrung her hands. "Please tell me I heard wrong?" she whispered.

A bizarre heat wave of wickedness descended over Kate in the presence of the older woman's profound goodness. From her re-pinned but still disheveled hair, to the musky moisture between her thighs and her swollen, just-kissed lips.

Blaine blew out a slow breath, but before he had to lie on her behalf, Kate said, "You didn't hear wrong." Her hand was amazingly steady as she tucked some hair behind her ear. "You know me as Kate. But my working name is Brandy."

Elaine's eyes filled with an emotion that looked too much like sorrow, or perhaps even bitter disappointment. "I...see."

Kate—no, Brandy—she'd always be Brandy with a client, felt Blaine's stare on her. She fought for calm and somehow managed to speak with a poise she certainly didn't feel. "I'm a paid escort."

*And your son is my best client.*

Elaine's face paled a little more. She sent a disbelieving stare Blaine's way. "And you're okay with that?"

She sensed him stiffen beside her. "What choice do I have?" He was nothing if not honest. "I want Kate for myself. But at the end of the day, it's totally her decision."

Brandy reined in a sudden desire to surrender to expectations, to become Blaine's mistress and the woman who'd feel lucky indeed to have a man like him obsessed with her. But she'd learned a long time ago it wasn't ever in her best interests to be a carbon copy of someone else.

She wasn't prepared to give up her way of life to please everyone else. Not if there was a big chance her sacrifice would be in vain. Not if there was a chance she'd be left trying to stick back together the pieces of her broken heart.

She tilted her chin. "I'm sorry, Elaine. I know you're upset, but I won't put my fate into anyone else's hands but my own."

Elaine's voice cracked. "I was just so sure you two belonged together."

It was strange how utterly helpless she felt and how much she wanted to comfort this woman who'd shown her nothing but kindness. She had shattered Elaine's hopes for grandchildren...at least until Blaine found someone else, someone far more suitable for the role.

The pain that went through her chest at the thought wasn't something she wanted to explore right now. It was akin to grieving. Intense and bewildering.

Then Blaine took Kate's hand in his and bent close to her ear. "Don't ever be sorry, not to anyone. Not even to me. When we get together, it's because it's the right thing for you, too."

*When?*

Despite the fact he'd all but disregarded her announcement to end things between them, she had an insane urge to melt against him and accept anything he proposed, even if only for a short time. But then he lifted her hand and kissed her knuckles, releasing her before stepping toward his mother.

"I'm sorry our evening didn't go the way you hoped it would."

Brandy closed herself off from whatever his mother said in return. After coming so damn close to surrendering everything for Blaine, she had to prepare herself for a future without him in it.

A future that would no longer shine half as brightly.

# Chapter Seven

**B**laine stole another glance at Kate as he drove through his mother's suburb. His headlights swept over a tree-lined park, where in daylight hours, a lake teemed with geese and ducks.

Where people walked along the paths, and families had picnics at the park tables while children scampered in the playground. He could imagine doing all those things and more with Kate one day, if only he could break through her walls. But he'd come to the conclusion that some walls were simply meant to be scaled.

He had to scramble up those walls even faster now that she'd admitted to wanting to break things off. Because he was determined Kate wasn't going anywhere. He was merciless at getting what he wanted, and she was at the top of his most wanted list.

His belly clenched. Losing Kate wasn't even an option.

He flicked on the indicator and headed back south on the highway. "So what did you think of my mother?"

She took her time answering. "I thought she was lovely and warm…"

"But?" he prompted.

"But I think she hates me."

"She'd never hate you." How could anyone hate his Kate? She was beautiful inside and out, a shining light in a world that too often revealed its murkier side. "Believe me when I say it's only your profession she dislikes."

She stiffened. "Unfortunately my profession is a big part of who I am."

He nodded, torn between despising the profession that meant other men knew her as intimately as he did, and being thankful her profession meant she was attainable to someone like him. "Give my mother some time. She has good reason to feel the way she does."

"Oh?"

He stared ahead, though he couldn't help but deliberate over Kate's interest. If she really wanted to break their arrangement, why was she even interested in hearing about his mother?

More importantly, when was Kate going to allow herself to trust? To love? To give herself the go-ahead for happiness? And to realize she deserved a life that didn't center solely on her looks and being amazing in bed.

Not that he'd complain about any of those facts. It was her looks, after all, that drew him to her in the first place. But even then, he'd seen beyond all that to the beautiful woman beneath. She radiated goodness and innocence, despite her career choice. Or perhaps, because of it.

She was such an enigma—sex and purity all rolled up into one gorgeous package. And he couldn't get enough of her.

He squinted against oncoming, over-bright headlights, taking a moment to focus on the present and tell her a little about his not-so-great role model of a parent. "My father enjoyed squandering money we didn't have on things he shouldn't have wanted. He died sharing a bed with three prostitutes, and with more drugs and alcohol in his system than his heart could take."

A streetlight flashed past, showing Kate's profile as she lifted a hand to her mouth. "That's terrible. I'm so sorry Blaine."

He wanted anything *but* pity from her, and his voice came out gruff when he said, "Don't be. He was a good-for-nothing player, addicted to sex and drugs. Frankly, I'm ashamed to have been related to him."

"You know you're nothing like him," she said gently. "You'll be a wonderful husband and father one day."

He'd had concerns that he might take after his father's side when it came to paid sex, but he realized now it was Kate who was his one and only addiction. She was all he'd ever want or need.

He glanced her way. "And one day, you'll be a great wife and mother." He wanted with a quiet desperation to be that man who made her all those things and more.

It turned his stomach to imagine her with someone else, someone who was a permanent part of her life. Almost as much as it tore him up a little more each day knowing she was an escort who other men paid for her services.

She sighed. "Yeah well, I'm not sure I'll ever be a wife *or* a mother."

He frowned. Did she realize how great she'd be in that role? It'd be a travesty for her to never know the wonder of being a mother, never realize the love of one man...him.

She might be a high-class escort, but was she actually selling herself short?

"You deserve to find great love and share the experience of having children," he said hoarsely. Damn, she deserved that and so much more.

She laughed, but he didn't hear any joy in the sound. "I've seen the devastation left behind by marriage. I'm not ready to go down that path yet, if ever."

His frown deepened. What had happened in her family that made her find the whole marriage thing so distasteful? He'd uncovered her medical records and some basic facts, which had included some bullying issues she'd dealt with in her youth. But maybe it was past time he learned a whole lot more and delved deeper into her past?

He blew out a slow breath. He *needed* to know more about her, find out what it was that made her tick, why she was so afraid to trust. Maybe then he could unravel the tangle around her heart and expose a love just waiting to be found.

As he turned off the highway and headed toward the little Italian restaurant on the outskirts of Sydney, he made a mental note to contact the private investigation firm he'd used more than a few times in the past. If Kate had anything to hide, he'd find it.

Even before he pulled into the car-park of the quaint stone façade cottage, he knew Lorenzo, the owner of the establishment—or at least, the part-owner if one looked closely enough at the books—would love Kate. But then, Lorenzo was a ladies' man who was particularly fond of gorgeous blondes.

Once inside, the restaurant's cozy ambience was showcased by a fireplace burning cheerily in a nook over on the far side of the room. Squat, red candles glowed behind intricate glass holders on little tables with white tablecloths. Waitresses in red dress uniforms and little aprons moved around the room, taking orders and delivering food.

Kate took an appreciative sniff. "It smells wonderful in here."

He nodded. "It sure does." Lorenzo also had a fondness for garlic and onions. Blaine smirked. It was a pity those same ladies Lorenzo loved didn't appreciate his garlicky breath nearly as much.

Lorenzo himself appeared in his chef whites, his skin swarthy and his dark moustache graying a little at the ends. He swept a dramatic bow to Kate, who giggled at the visual dramatics. "It's a pleasure to finally meet the woman who appears to have set my friend's heart aflutter." Lorenzo sent him a bemused look. "I never thought I'd see the day."

Blaine nodded. "Stranger things have happened, I'm sure."

Lorenzo vehemently shook his dark head. "Not in my time." He turned back to Kate and gave her an appreciative up-and-down look. "But I can certainly see why."

After Lorenzo took them to a private table that sat in a raised alcove all on its own, he handed them a menu with a flourish and said, "The specials of the day are the prawn and scallop pizza, or chicken and mushroom fettuccini."

Kate looked at Blaine. "Yum."

Lorenzo chuckled. "A woman after my own heart. I'll give you a few minutes to have a look at the menu before I take your orders. I'll send a drinks waitress over shortly."

Blaine watched Kate scan the menu, her love of good food more than apparent. Was she a gym junkie or did a great metabolism keep her in such gorgeous shape?

*Or maybe it's all the hot and sweaty sex*, a snide voice offered.

He squeezed his eyes shut for a moment, dragging back some level of sanity even as he recognized he really did know too little about his Kate. And right or wrong, he'd spend his whole fortune, if need be, to find out everything about her, to solve her trust issues.

Kate put down the menu. "I think I might go with the chicken and mushroom fettuccini special."

He nodded. "That sounds good." There was nothing quite like home-style Italian cooking done really well. "I'm going with the veal marsala."

After they chose a bottle of wine to share and Lorenzo had taken their order, Blaine leaned across the table and took her hand in his, snaring her gaze with his own. "There's something I really need to know."

Her expression immediately shut down, but as much as he hated to put a dampener on the mood, this couldn't be put off any longer.

"Oh?" she said faintly.

"Why do you want us to stop seeing each other?"

She bit into her bottom lip. "You want to discuss this now?"

"Is there ever a good time to hear bad news?" he countered.

Her eyes softened, the chatter from other diners fading away when she said, "We're getting too close."

"And that scares you?" he asked gently.

She blinked. "It's against the agency rules for a client and call girl to become...a couple."

The very idea of them being together in every sense of the word made his heart beat accelerate, his perceptions heighten, until he was aware of every changing nuance of her expression. "Do you want to know what I think?" he said carefully, though something primal and possessive screamed to be unleashed. "I think you're pushing me away because real and genuine intimacy terrifies you."

At her widening eyes, he knew he'd hit a nerve. But she was saved from answering when their wine arrived. The waitress took her time uncorking and pouring them each a flute. Kate took a good-sized swallow before she answered.

"Business is business. I need to keep that totally separate from my personal life."

He brushed a hand along her cheek, loving her silky-soft skin and flawless complexion. "So what do *you* really want?" he asked.

She frowned. "What do you mean?"

His hand moved to cup her chin, keeping her stare level with his. "Do you want to keep our relationship business or personal? Because I *know* you don't want to break things off any more than I do." He leaned forward, allowing the heat of his gaze to burn through. "Either way, I'm not letting you go."

Her mouth dropped open, and for a moment her eyes reflected the burn in his stare. Then she pulled free from his clasp and drained the last of the wine from her glass. "You know, there are some things in this world that are unattainable, even for someone like you."

He cocked his head to the side. "Everyone has a price."

She flushed, and shook her head slowly. "My career is all I have. I won't let you take that away from me."

Blaine felt the blood drain from his face. Out of all the things she could have said, *that* wasn't one of them. Jesus Christ, was sleeping with men for money her one and only ambition? Or had she been so screwed over in the past that she imagined it was all she wanted from life?

It only reinforced his growing need to dig into her history.

A bowl of pasta was placed in front of Kate. Once his veal dish was put down, he nodded a distracted thanks. But he didn't drag his stare away from Kate to notice the waiter—Lorenzo?—discreetly disappear. Right now, Kate was all he cared about...all he ever cared about.

Of course, being that he was a silent partner in Lorenzo's business helped to solidify Blaine's privacy.

He pulled in a steadying breath, putting a halt to words that were better left unsaid. He'd fought dirty to get where he was in the corporate world, but maybe turning a cold shoulder from that tried and true method was where he'd gone wrong with Kate?

Resolve filled him. No more wearing kid gloves. No more baby steps around her. He wouldn't even tell her that he'd already managed to book her in for tomorrow night—at a princely sum—to see her again.

It was past time to make things happen.

# Chapter Eight

Kate sipped on her flat white coffee as the voices of Claire, Natalie and Eloise—otherwise known in the escort industry as Scarlet, Tiffany and Savannah—washed over her.

She was too distracted and wound up today to enjoy the company of her friends. Not only because her thoughts returned again and again to the pleasure Blaine had dragged from her body last night after he'd taken her to his home. She was as much consumed by thoughts of the looming night ahead, and was both exhilarated and sickened knowing she'd be with Blaine yet again.

She'd somehow found the strength last night to say goodbye once and for all to him, only to have the VIP Agency ring this morning and tell her that he'd secured yet another booking with her.

Blaine was right—their intimacy did seriously scare her—but what really frightened her was how effortlessly he thwarted her attempts to break free. She was too soft when it came to him. Too weak to even put up a fight against being with him again.

She hadn't even protested when Maisey had told her the news. She'd been too stunned to do anything but murmur a monosyllable response. She could only imagine how much Blaine had paid for the VIP Agency to break her next client's contract.

"Hello. Earth to Kate. Anyone home?"

At Natalie's voice, Kate brought her focus back to the present. "Sorry, I was a million miles away."

Natalie blinked long, dark lashes, for a second obscuring her gorgeous icy-blue stare. It didn't stop the look of knowing from falling across her face. "You can say that again." She tossed a chunk of long, blonde hair behind a slender shoulder. "So tell us...who is the lucky man?"

Eloise winked. "Or maybe it's who are the lucky *men*?"

Claire's dry laugh lacked its usual warmth. "C'mon Eloise, we all know your obsession with the Wolfe brothers. It doesn't mean we all get to lust after two guys."

Eloise shrugged, her exotic dark eyes twinkling with mischief and something a little bit mysterious. "Hey, what can I say? They're both gorgeous and great in bed. It's a win-win."

Kate managed a smile, despite the seriousness of her thoughts. Despite the fact that she shared more than a little of Claire's inner turmoil for a client. "I'm not so sure the man in question is lucky." She sighed. "The rules are simple enough. We can't have a relationship outside the bedroom with our clients."

"Or two clients," Claire added with a pointed look Eloise's way.

Eloise's grin all but lit up the coffee shop. "Who said anything about a relationship?"

Kate blew out a slow breath. "Be careful Eloise, it's all too easy for excitement and fun to slide into something more serious."

Claire nodded commiseration even as Natalie put a hand over Kate's. "Please tell me you're not falling for a client? Out of all of us, you're the most level headed and career orientated."

Kate's smile turned into a grimace. The girls knew her too well. A pity she'd lost sight of that part of herself somewhere along the way. "I'm honestly not sure what my feelings are for him anymore."

*Liar! You only want to break things off with him because you're already in too deep.*

Claire leaned forward in her seat, her striking flame-red hair piled into its usual topknot. "Do you have butterflies in the stomach every time he's booked you for the night?"

Eloise wound a strand of inky-black hair around a finger. "Do you want to have sex with them—ah, *him*—above anyone else?"

Natalie added, "Do you wish you'd met him under entirely different circumstances?"

Kate leaned back in her seat, eyeing each of her stunning friends with a whole new perspective. "So I'm guessing I'm not alone in questioning my feelings, then?"

Claire sighed. "Well I think it's safe to say we all know what I think about a particular man."

Eloise shook her head. "Not me. Honestly, I'm too selfish to fall for anyone. I left behind subjugation when I emigrated here from Nepal with my family, and I refuse to give all that away by allowing a man to rule my life."

Kate hadn't heard much about Eloise's life before she became an escort, and though she was intrigued, none of the girls ever pushed for personal information. But it didn't mean the one girl who hadn't voiced anything further was off the hook. She turned to Natalie. "What about you?"

The blonde woman flushed, and looked away. "Even if I did have...feelings for someone, I refuse to act on them."

Kate nodded. "I can relate."

Natalie looked back, her eyes flashing blue fire. "Actually, I doubt any of you do." She sighed heavily. "The man I'm fighting *not* to have feelings for is seventeen years my senior and...married."

Kate stared. Everyone stared. It wasn't unusual for a married man to request their services. In fact, it was all too common. But to imagine that same married man would return deep feelings for an escort...it just didn't happen.

Eloise pushed back her chair and stood, her midnight-black hair in vivid contrast to her cropped white blouse and green denim shorts. "Well, I don't know about anyone else, but I think a little retail therapy wouldn't go astray."

Claire nodded. "I'm keen for that."

Natalie sucked in a breath and then smiled at Kate. "Yes. Let's go have some fun."

Blaine disconnected from the four-way teleconference, his mind only half on the job. Since when had corporate takeovers become so damn mundane and lackluster?

Taking on a new company and shaping it to his exacting standards to make it successful had become his trademark. One he wasn't about to fail at now, despite his sudden disinterest.

A knock sounded on the hazy pearl-colored glass door of his office. "Come in," he called out, smoothing away any signs of displeasure from his face.

Lately everything had lost a little of its sheen, until the moment he was reunited with Kate. Then everything was bright and sharp, and filled with wonder. Like watching an old black-and-white television, then blinking to see a plasma color television for the first time and having everything come to glorious life.

Samantha, his secretary cum personal assistant, walked into his office, a woman on a mission. "Is everything okay with you lately?" she asked crisply, all business as per usual. Exactly the reason he'd hired her.

He arched a brow even as he smothered a telling smile. "Shouldn't it be?"

Sam's usually composed face wilted into a frown. "With your latest acquisition, I should think so. If only you weren't so distracted."

He shrugged. "That obvious, huh?"

She sighed, her cool blue stare softening a little. "I never thought I'd see the day when a woman would snare you in her web"

He loosened the knot in his tie, feeling suddenly suffocated by the damn thing. "Yeah, well, now I just have to convince her she can't live without me, either."

It was Sam's turn to arch a brow, before she placed a stack of paperwork on his desk. "Here are all the documents you requested from last month's merger."

Bloody hell. Reading all the small print before signing on the dotted line wasn't something he felt close to capable of doing right now. Not when his thoughts were consumed by Kate. But he wasn't going to relent this once and put all his faith in a lawyer. No, his work ethic and attention to detail weren't going to suffer because of his disarrayed emotions.

Nothing could be left to chance. He wouldn't take three steps back after working his ass off to take two steps forward. He dropped his hand, breathing much more freely as he picked up the first page. He'd read the contract thoroughly, then he'd devote all his attention to Kate later tonight.

Somehow convince her that what they had was real and long-lasting, if she'd only open herself up and trust in him.

Sam sighed loudly into the silence. "All I know for sure is that you've left behind a trail of lovesick and heart-sore women who are even now desperate for your attention. Yet it looks as though you've chosen possibly the one woman on Earth, besides me," she elaborated with a smirk, "who doesn't share your same feelings." Her smirk grew a fraction. "I really must meet her."

Blaine ignored the fine print blurring before his eyes to send her a wry look. "So you can congratulate her on leading me around by my short and curlies?"

His secretary's restraint had to be legendary, as she kept a straight face and said sweetly, "Let's just say she must be someone pretty special."

He watched Sam close his office door behind her, before he said softly, "Yes, she most certainly is."

# Chapter Nine

**I**t felt strange stepping out of the car to a blaze of outside lights, as though Blaine wanted to now proclaim her arrival to the world.

So much for discretion.

Nerves knotted in her belly at the coming confrontation.

At the night ahead.

At its ending.

Her hand tightened on her fire-red clutch purse, the same color as her gauzy halter-neck dress that flared out from the waist. She shivered. She couldn't help but acknowledge that tonight would be memorable...life changing. And not in a good way.

Blaine wouldn't give her up, not without a fight.

Her heels clacked on the granite path as she approached the same red door as the night before. Except this time her smile was forced and her belly churned with trepidation. Aside from physical release, there was little to look forward to tonight.

Amazing the difference a few days could make.

Blaine swung the door open before she'd reached it. She swallowed, her heart fluttering. He looked divine, his fitted tux showcasing his height, his lean but muscled breadth.

"Hi," she said huskily, self-conscious somehow at his lingering appraisal.

"Stunning," he murmured in return.

For one dizzying moment, she wondered if perhaps he'd looked beyond her outer layer to the beauty within. But then he claimed her mouth with his own in a slow, leisurely exploration of lips and tongue, and the idea melted away.

No. He simply wanted the one woman he'd soon no longer have. Besides, successful men like Blaine didn't care so much for inner beauty, did they? Her own father had been proof of that.

She stiffened and pulled away first. Damn it. Some memories should never be taken out of the closet. And she had to stop judging every man by her father's behavior. Blaine was nothing like him. Not that it mattered either way, not after tonight. She took a step back, her top teeth worrying into her bottom lip. "Someone might see us."

Blaine's eyes blazed, passionate and possessive. "Let them."

When he pulled her back the next time, his mouth, as it claimed hers once again, alternated between soft and coaxing, then hard and demanding. She sighed into his mouth, drowning in a sea of sensation. Thoughts no longer entered her consciousness. Nothing penetrated the world he took her to, except just how badly she wanted him.

All of him.

Minutes later they broke apart. His face, as he looked down at her, was stamped with a fierce intensity that bordered on alarming. He appeared every inch the big, bad wolf who wanted to eat her. Then he smiled and stepped away. She sucked in an unsteady breath, her heartbeat stabilizing and her renewed anxiety lifting.

His hard-edged exterior too often hid the adoring, romantic man she'd seen more and more often of late. Yet, despite her professional side screaming that things were becoming way too personal and way too intense, she'd basked in his attention.

Had. Past tense.

"We have a few minutes," he said smoothly. "Would you care for a drink?"

She nodded, forcing a smile. "I'd love one."

Two snifters of brandy were already poured and waiting on the bar in his entertainment room. He handed one to her and she cupped it in the palm of her hand, swirling the liquid around and around, and watching the firelight refracted in its depths.

Blaine raised his drink in a toast, a slightly crooked smile curling his lips. "To us."

She raised hers too, a little more awkwardly and feeling ill-at-ease, knowing "us" wouldn't be a part of the equation for much longer. Despite herself, the thought left her sick at heart.

Blaine's eyes captured hers as he added deliberately, "May there be many more nights the same as this one."

*That's one wish that won't be coming true.*

She wouldn't speak her thoughts out loud. Not when she was supposed to be his every fantasy come true. Instead, she tossed back her drink, needing its fortification. The brandy burned all the way down her throat, creating a pleasant warmth in her belly and a surge of affirmation in her breast. She returned her empty glass to the bar. "So it's party before pleasure?"

Placing his glass beside hers, he clasped her hips and tugged her close. "Pleasure first," he corrected softly, holding her stare.

Her breath came out in a surprised hiss when he spun her around to face the mirror, her spine pressed against his chest, his flat belly and the thick wedge of his arousal.

Her face was already flushed with passion, the tight upsweep of her strawberry-blonde hair ready to tumble past her shoulders in utter abandonment and disarray. Not unlike her emotions.

"But you'll be the only one coming," he added in an undertone.

She swallowed. Hard.

Blaine never ceased to excite her, never ceased to make her want him even more than before. But she couldn't afford what this would do to her...to them. Her eyes connected to his in the mirror. Saying goodbye to him was going to be the hardest thing she'd ever done.

His stare narrowed, sharp, possessive. "Are you wearing any underwear?"

She nodded, as helpless as a mouse in the presence of a cobra. "A thong and garters," she managed, her voice whisper-soft.

"Good." His hands moved downward from her hips, lifting the petal-like skirt of her dress.

His touch was hot between her thighs. When he pushed aside the scrap of lace that was her thong to expose her pussy, she all but collapsed against him, her bones turning to liquid.

"You'll climax for me," he said hoarsely, "then every time you walk, every time you sit or stand tonight, you'll be aware of the wetness down there."

His breath touched her ear at about the same time his fingers parted her flesh. "Every time someone comes near and smells your aroma, they will know you are mine."

*Oh. Fuck.*

If words were an aphrodisiac, then he was the master. She was close to convulsing with pleasure even before one of his fingers massaged the aching gem of her clit. Over and over again. Until she was writhing and grinding against him, her head resting against his chest. His golden, glittering eyes held hers, watching as her breath abruptly caught, her body jerking with release, then trembling with the after effects.

"I must be a fool for not filling your pussy and fucking you senseless, my seed spilling inside you," he said throatily.

She was incapable of answering and recovering any semblance of the upper hand. She didn't even have the energy to mention that any more sex between them would be with a condom sheathing his cock. Instead she said weakly, "Your romantic words get me every time."

"Perhaps I'm saving the romance for later, hmm?"

She pulled free from his embrace, the intensity of his stare causing her to feel uneasy. She looked away and adjusted her thong, her dress, before she gathered up her clutch purse and took his proffered hand.

～

The party was at the Sydney Opera House, with beautiful views of the harbor and its myriad twinkling lights along the shoreline.

She sneaked a glance behind them. "No bodyguards tonight?"

"No. Believe it or not, we're safer amongst a crowd."

A handful of musicians had set up beside a raised stage and a makeshift dance floor. They played cover songs, and a popular ballad was lending a little more cheer to the rich, stuffy atmosphere.

The women in their sequined gowns and flashing jewels made Brandy feel underdressed. But as if reading her thoughts, Blaine said in an undertone, "Your simple, stunning elegance has already drawn the eye of every man in the room."

She shivered a little, recognizing he meant every word. Yes, they were attracting a lot of attention, but it was from the women as much as the men, their envious glances sliding between her and the delicious man by her side.

Even without all his wealth and good looks, there was something magnetic about Blaine that drew the eye. He carried himself with an inborn assurance and self-belief she secretly envied and admired in equal measure.

Blaine took two drinks from a passing waiter before handing one to her. She murmured thanks, the bubbly effervescence that slid down her throat lending her a little more courage.

She could handle herself in social situations, although formal affairs such as these left her feeling inadequate, as though she didn't belong. She could only hope she appeared poised and confident on the outside.

Blaine introduced her to one group of people after another until she lost track of the number of important and influential guests with whom he was on first-name basis. Then he drew her toward the next group.

*Oh. Shit.*

"Brandy, I'd like you to meet Calvin and his wife, Sharlene."

Her eyes fixed on Calvin. She kept all her shock on the inside as she allowed him—a former client—to take her hand and press fleshy lips to her knuckles.

"What a pleasure," he said with a drawling smirk, his nostrils flaring as though he really was aware of the musky scent between her thighs.

Except that she had a bad feeling the scent only emphasized his adverse opinion of her. The same man she'd rejected when his fetish for rough, violent sex had become apparent. He'd also been the man who'd fast-tracked her into becoming more selective with her clients.

"Kate? Oh my god…is that really you?"

Even before she tugged her hand free to turn toward Calvin's wife, she knew who she'd face. Brandy would remember that voice anywhere. A class-A bitch and spoiled rich kid, all of Sharlene's prettiness had just happened to be on the outside. Her inner ugliness hadn't stopped her from being the most popular girl in high school.

The same woman who'd made her life a living hell.

"It really is you!" Sharlene looked her up and down with frank and disbelieving envy. "You look amazing."

The other woman could say that now. And little wonder. Age hadn't done Sharlene any favors—or maybe her husband was as nasty out of bed as he was in it, infecting those around him with his own personal brand of ugliness?

Sharlene's face twitched into what should have been a frown, if only her obviously wrinkle-free, Botoxed features allowed such movement. "Why the name change?"

Calvin guffawed, his heavy jaw made more noticeable with his obnoxious laugh. He lifted a shoulder that was still as broad and heavy as it was in his linebacker days when he'd lived in the states. His career was one thing he'd managed to boast about in their short time together. "Sweetheart, use your imagination. In her line of work, she needs to be anonymous for her own safety."

Brandy felt the blood drain right out of her face even as Blaine stiffened beside her.

It was ironic that the one man she had feared the most referred to her line of work as being dangerous.

Sharlene's eyes rounded with evident realization before she clapped a hand to her mouth. "No. Way! Kate. Ah, Brandy, is that true?" She leaned forward, clearly titillated when she hissed, "You're a whore?"

And just like that, something within Brandy shut down. One well-aimed hit to the solar plexus and she was the shy plain Jane with no friends and all too many insecurities.

Blaine put his arm around her rigid shoulders and drew her close, shielding her from harm. She wilted against him. This once, she could only be thankful for the security he offered.

Later...much later, she'd be strong again.

Blaine's gaze held Sharlene's as he challenged softly, "Define whore?"

The other woman shrank a little at the clear warning in his voice, and its undertone of distaste. Brandy released an unsteady breath. How easily he'd switched all the ugliness back onto Calvin's wife.

Blaine swung away from Sharlene, who was grappling for a suitable reply. His attention was now on the man who'd forgotten the meaning of discretion in order to settle a score. "Tell me, Calvin. How is it that you know so much about Brandy?"

Sharlene turned to her husband with sudden uncertainty in her eyes. "What is going on, Calvin? How *do* you know her?"

Brandy leaned further into Blaine's strong body, feeding off his strength just a little longer, before deciding enough was enough. The time for being strong was here and now, not later. If she could find the strength within to leave Blaine, then standing up to these two should be a walk in the park.

She stepped out of Blaine's arms. "Actually we have met." When Sharlene threw her a glaring look of disbelief, she added, "Except I didn't much care for his penchant for violence."

If Calvin roughed up his spouse in the same way he did his escorts, Sharlene would get her drift. And going by the other woman's stifled gasp, it was clear she did.

Sympathy for Sharlene, and the life she must share with this man, softened any ill will toward her. Brandy could only hope the nasty displeasure stamped into every hard crevice on Calvin's face, wouldn't mean that his wife would later take the brunt of his anger. But his focus wasn't on his wife. It was all on her.

A pulse beat into life at his temple, his hands curling into fists. "Listen to me, you little—"

"I believe we have a meeting early next week," Blaine said in an undertone that somehow oozed authority right along with the threat of reprisal.

Calvin pulled himself together, at least outwardly. He all but bowed to the alpha male when he nodded stiffly and said, "I'll be there."

Blaine looked anything but appeased. "See that you are." When he took her arm once again and escorted her away from the pair of piranhas, he murmured, "Are you okay?"

She looked up at his taut face. "I'm fine. I've dealt with worse."

Calvin had seen to that. He'd reminded her that her father wasn't the only man in the world who was an asshole.

# Chapter Ten

**B**laine's eyes narrowed, dangerously assessing. "Your job?"

She shivered, aware that Blaine was far more lethal than anything Calvin could muster. But she didn't answer, didn't feel the need to explain herself or her chosen career. Her silence seemed answer enough.

His mouth tightened. "You know you don't need to do what you're doing. Not anymore."

She inhaled sharply. He didn't need to say the words, didn't need to tell her he'd look after her. But why did he think being his mistress would be so much better? She'd still be getting paid for sex, the only difference being that it would be with one man.

And then what?

Nothing. She'd be right back to square one the moment he'd had enough of her.

No. She couldn't rely on anyone but herself. She'd already learned that the hard way.

As though knowing he'd pushed her far enough, Blaine changed tactics and asked, "Would you care to dance?"

The dance floor was empty, but sensing Sharlene's and Calvin's eyes still boring into her back, she knew she needed to fight fire with fire. Screw them. Let them watch. She wasn't going to make excuses. She loved sex, loved her job. She wasn't going to let another person's judgments make her feel inferior or ashamed in any way.

When were men like Calvin going to realize they paid their unhappy wives a whole hell of a lot more than any call girl to satisfy their needs?

She lifted her chin. Better to stay than run scared. "I'd love to."

His eyes glinted with satisfaction and something else, something not quite definable, when he smiled and she stepped into his arms. Her belly fluttered. Sometimes she swore she glimpsed more than lust in Blaine's stare, something much deeper than even his desire to possess her. She had to constantly remind herself she was a call girl, and that men rarely saw beyond that label.

No matter that Blaine thought he wanted a longer-term arrangement, she'd still be nothing more than a paid mistress. She wasn't girlfriend material. She'd gone into the business with her eyes wide open, aware of what she was getting into.

She'd made her bed...

A slow melody started up, but Brandy scarcely noticed. She was too attuned to Blaine and his strong feelings for her. His interest was the last thing she needed, especially knowing this was their last night together. Somehow it didn't stop the glow from spreading inside.

She pushed away all reservation, and instead concentrated on following Blaine's lead. He was a fabulous dancer. While she'd had enough lessons to make her passable in any given situation, she knew with Blaine in charge, they moved fluidly across the floor, his big, adept hand on the bared skin of her back, her skirts swishing.

And all the while, dozens of admiring eyes followed them.

She looked up at Blaine's determined stare. Is this what he really wanted? Did he hope people would see them as a couple? She frowned. He might want her as a mistress, but surely it'd be the downfall of his celebrated career if others got wind of who he was really with?

Evidently he didn't care.

"You want to talk about it?" he asked, his head bent and his voice brushing over her ear.

She ignored the instant raise of goosebumps. "What do you mean?"

"That exchange between you and Calvin...not to mention his wife."

She shrugged, keeping her tone light, casual. "Calvin was a client."

The tightening of Blaine's hands confirmed his possessiveness. It also reconfirmed her decision to part ways with him before things got even more serious.

As though perceiving her thoughts, he visibly relaxed, his touch gentling. "Go on."

She shrugged. "And Sharlene was someone I knew in high school."

"A friend?"

Her short burst of laughter held no trace of humor. "Hardly. She was more an enemy who made my life miserable in every way."

The song came to an end.

They stilled. Neither moved as another ballad swept over them.

Blaine's hands tightened fractionally as he stared down at her. "She felt threatened by you." Before she could disabuse him of that absurd idea, he added, "Life has a funny way of evening scores."

"I know." She sighed. "I can't believe I'm saying this, but I almost feel sorry for her being married to that...pig."

"He's that bad?"

She nodded, her mouth drying at his intense look. "Worse."

His face tightened. "Then I'll be certain he knows never to go near you again."

She pulled back and shook her head. "I can take care of myself."

His stare darkened. "Is it really so bad to have someone want to look out for you?"

Yearning once again pulled at her defenses. She gritted her teeth, refusing to give in to his arrangement that would be unattainable long-term. Besides, she'd fought hard for her independence, and she wasn't about to hand those reins—and that kind of power—over to someone else.

About to put her thoughts into words, a well-coiffed matron with sky-high heels and heavy earrings mounted the nearby stage and took hold of the microphone. "First of all, I want to thank you, one and all, for coming tonight and making this awareness fundraiser a resounding success." As a polite round of applause dimmed, she added with a beaming smile, "But I'm sure you are all hungry. Please take your designated seats and enjoy your meals while our guest speakers entertain you."

Blaine took her hand and guided her through the throng of people to the round table for two close to the stage.

"I'm the keynote speaker," he informed her at seeing her arched brow.

After he pulled out her chair, then seated himself, she leaned in close and said softly, "Then perhaps I should have asked what this charity fundraiser is all about?"

He nodded toward the stage. "You're about to find out."

A young woman with long, mouse-brown hair and an even more timid demeanor stepped onto the stage. Although her voice shook, it was obvious how bad her childhood had been as she recounted her days spent terrorized by schoolyard bullies.

The first course arrived, some kind of consommé in a delicate, chalk-white bowl. Brandy didn't touch it. All her attention was centered on the young woman whose past sounded so similar to her own.

She was half aware of Blaine's considering gaze on her, but this once she ignored his regard. The woman's speech was poignant and sad. Worse, it brought back memories like a reopened wound, fresh and painful. And more than a little confronting.

When the woman on stage concluded by admitting that as a teen she'd attempted to take her own life, Brandy's throat clogged, her vision misting over. The woman might be timid, but she had the heart of a lion. Not only had she faced her fears, she spoke about them in the hopes that others would be saved from the turmoil she'd gone through.

Brandy wilted against her seat as the speaker left the stage as quietly as she'd arrived. Where would her own life have taken her without the threat of school bullies to contend with? She most certainly would have coped with her mother's death a whole lot better if she'd had true friends around her to comfort and offer solace, even share a little of her pain and grief.

Would she have been confident in her own right, without the admiration of a man to make her feel complete? She glanced at Blaine. Would she have been lucky enough to marry someone like him? Or would she have forged ahead in some other, more acceptable career, and taken on someone like him as a lover instead?

Her belly tightened. The woman on stage had been strong enough to make serious changes in her life. Was it possible she too could change direction from the path she'd chosen? More importantly, did she *want* to put her trust in a man, in Blaine, and make those changes?

The next speaker was announced when Blaine tilted his head close to her, his voice feathering across her earlobe. "We're funding a national campaign aimed at putting an end to bullying."

She sucked in a steadying breath, but it didn't stop the odd sensation from taking over her body. It was as if tonight she'd been brought full circle and the universe was pointing her in a whole new direction. Her belly fluttered. It was now her decision whether to follow those signposts...or not.

Dare she hope for a future with Blaine? Was it possible to find happiness with one man? For one man to find happiness with her? Surely all the long-lived marriages around the globe proved it was a plausible conclusion.

Blaine signaled for a waiter who immediately came over and filled her empty wine glass. She took a mouthful, barely noticing its extravagant flavor. Barely registering the monotone voice of the man who'd taken to the stage.

"I didn't thank you," Blaine said in a whisper.

She turned to him, his open warmth and adoration producing an ache somewhere in the vicinity of her chest. Her mind scrambled to make sense of it all even as lightheadedness assailed her. This was all wrong! Blaine didn't love her! Of course he didn't.

So why was she drowning in a sea of denial, and he was the lifesaver with an outstretched hand?

"Wh...what for?" she managed.

"For accepting my invitation tonight. And taking a chance on us."

Her mouth dried. But before she could respond, the coiffed woman once again took the microphone and announced Blaine's name.

He pressed a reassuring kiss to her scalp before brushing a lingering hand across her shoulder. Moments later, he stood and took the stage.

She gulped in some air, focusing on Blaine to steady her nerves. The non-fantasy part of her brain stepped in, logical and reasonable. Blaine wanted her to be his mistress. That. Was. It. Only when her breathing returned to some semblance of normality, did she perceive her anxiety attack had slowly seeped away, like it'd never been.

*I'm happy on my own. I don't need a man permanently in my life to make things right.*

Yet all her attention stayed on Blaine, everything within her drawing strength from his commanding presence.

His gaze moved over the crowd as he introduced himself, his voice strong, authoritative. Captivating.

"Some of you might know me as a friend." He smiled, acknowledging a few of those in the seated audience. "Some as a business acquaintance. One thing I know for sure," he paused, holding the audience in the palm of his hand, "is that without you people, I'd never have become who I am today."

His stare locked with hers. She lifted her wine glass to her lips with an unsteady hand, draining it.

"I was once a young boy on the wrong side of the tracks, wanting desperately to prove my own worth. But for too long I allowed the influence and intimidation from older boys—seniors—to pull me right back down. Confronting my own self-doubt was the first major step..."

His voice warmed her, making her feel safe, secure. And more than a little dazed at knowing she wasn't alone, had never been alone in her pain. Little wonder she felt a deep connection to Blaine. He understood her in a way only someone who had experienced bullying could. Not only had he dragged himself out of the quagmire the bullies had tried to push him into he'd made a success of his life.

More than a success.

She barely heard the rest of his speech—he'd already touched her deeply—but knew it must have been rousing by the standing ovation he received.

When he returned to his seat, she'd already shrugged off the imaginary security blanket. Already ignored the signposts she's earlier glimpsed. She wouldn't be caught up in the emotions of the moment, wouldn't surrender her whole past like it'd never been.

She wouldn't make light of a history that had dictated her future.

The coiffed woman took the stage and thanked Blaine. As the applause finally died down, she brought the night's speeches to a close.

Brandy barely noticed. Not when Blaine took hold of her hand and pressed it to his chest...his heart.

*Oh god.*

She wanted only to bask in his warmth and generosity of spirit, wanted only to surrender to him completely. He might have played dirty in the past, but right now, all she saw was his goodness. She didn't have the strength to snatch her hand free. Instead she dropped her eyes from his, distanced herself emotionally.

"Kate?" he whispered hoarsely.

His saying her real name felt right on too many levels.

*Get a grip. He's your client, nothing else.*

Yet goosebumps erupted on her flesh even before she glanced back at his handsome-as-sin profile. Her pulses fluttered with both denial and need. She dragged back some semblance of rationality. He'd paid dearly for her tonight. She wouldn't let their finale be something easily forgotten.

She glanced at the main course a waiter presented to her. The aroma of crispy-skin duck was amazing, if only her belly didn't clench with rejection. Food was the last thing on her mind.

She leaned close to Blaine. "I don't know about you, but I'm not really hungry." Her free hand inched up his thigh at about the same time his breathing deepened. "At least not for food."

His eyes glinted, stark and needy. "I'll make the appropriate excuses as soon as I can and we'll head off."

She smiled, her hand lingering on his thigh. "Please...you eat. I need to use the ladies room."

Seeing the line-up of twittering ladies in the nearest restroom, she chose to walk to one she'd seen some distance from the function. Besides, the last thing she wanted right now was to brush aside the envious, sideward looks from any number of Blaine's admirers.

It would have only made it even more starkly apparent how easily he could replace her after tonight.

Minutes later, she was peering into the well-lit mirror, relishing the lack of female company as she uncapped her lipstick and reapplied a delicate smear of crimson to her lips.

She dropped her hand and took a step back, her green eyes sharpening as she assessed herself critically. She'd worked hard to keep herself toned, and at twenty-six years of age, she looked damn good. Skin lightly tanned, her figure slender but lush in all the right places.

Little wonder Sharlene didn't recognize her. No longer was she the cheaply clothed, self-conscious kid others noticed for all the wrong reasons. No longer did her grades matter, which had dropped alarmingly due to her many absences from school.

No longer did she feel unwanted.

Abandoned.

Inadequate.

The band started up another song, though it was faint from this distance. She dropped her lipstick back into her clutch bag. Time to return to the party. Time to go home with Blaine and end the night on a sexual high he wouldn't soon forget.

*Even once he is happily married with two point five kids?*

She pressed a hand to her belly as nausea rose fast inside.

Whatever she shared with Blaine...it had to stop. She'd never before wanted someone she couldn't have, never before lusted for a client beyond sex. She'd tucked away daydreams of a far different future a long time ago.

She'd chosen a life where the risk of being hurt was almost obsolete, as long as she didn't get close to anyone. As long as she didn't allow anyone to break through the walls around her heart.

Lost in thought, she didn't notice the reflection in the mirror behind her, didn't hear the footfalls until it was too late.

"Waiting for me, whore?"

# Chapter Eleven

**H**er breath came out in a rush as her eyes met Calvin's glittering, lust-filled stare. Her chest tightened, her pulse raced *Oh shit.* What had she been thinking? In her line of work, safety came first at all times. Instead, she'd been so busy thinking of ways to not think about Blaine, her welfare hadn't even registered.

"No." She tilted her chin, swallowing back the fear that froze her insides when she added scornfully, "You know I'm already with another client right now. And I don't do more than one man at a time."

"You're messing with me, right?" He stepped forward, two hundred and sixty pounds or more of bristling menace. "You fuck men for money. Since when do numbers come into the equation?"

Her breath hissed. The bastard knew that discretion and caution were part and parcel of her service. "Blaine has paid for my exclusive services. End of story."

"Exclusive?" His sneering voice caused fear to skid up and down her spine. "What would you know about the word? Or is Blaine brainwashing you into thinking you're too good now for someone like me?"

"Blaine is worth a hundred of you." With her heart in her throat, she tucked her bag under her arm and pushed past. "If you'll excuse me—"

"You're not excused, slut." He clamped onto her forearm with a meaty hand and hauled her against him. Her bag clattered to the floor and half the contents tumbled out. "You'll finish what we started last round—before you bailed on me."

Fear clawed at her innards when he ground the lump of his arousal against her belly. Right now, she wished desperately for the comings and goings of the chattering ladies in the restroom closer to the party. This far away, she could scream and no one would hear her. At least not now the band had started up again.

Calvin had her exactly where he wanted her.

And Blaine would probably assume she got waylaid or was taking her sweet time.

Damn. Shit. Fuck.

She had no choice for the moment but to play along.

She closed her eyes with a breathy and all-too-fake sigh of compliance. The egotistical bastard fell for it.

"That's better." His breath was hot and heavy on her face. "Play nice and you won't get hurt."

Fisting her hair, he pulled sharply. Bobby pins ripped free before tinkling across the tiled floor. Her hair tumbled down as tears sprang to her eyes. He yanked harder still, keeping her head back so that she was completely helpless in his grip.

"I mean to finish what we started," he said hoarsely. His free hand cupped one of her breasts and squeezed brutally. Her gasp ended in a whimper when he transferred his attention to her other breast, his fingers clamping onto her nipple and twisting. His loathsome smile reinforced the excited glint in his eyes. "Whether you want to or not."

She relaxed in his hold, forcing away all sensation of pain that lashed through her body. "I'll play nice if you do. Then I'll fuck you how I've always wanted to."

His mean eyes glazed over, his grip loosening a fraction. "You'd better mean that."

Idiot. The only head he was using right now was the one between his legs.

"Oh I do," she breathed. *Just wait and see.*

His voice came out thick. "Get on with it then." His fingers still bunched in her hair, he pressed her downward. "A blowjob first."

Yeah, she'd go down on him all right. But only so she could slam a fist into his family jewels—she hadn't been lying when she said she was going to fuck him just the way she wanted to.

Fuck him over.

She looked up and licked her lips. "I can't wait."

*And not in the way you think, asshole.*

"Dirty whore," he said hoarsely, splaying his thick thighs wide apart while she used deft fingers to undo his straining fly.

*Sick fuck.*

He'd pay for this, and not with his wallet. His pants and boxers dropped to his feet, his thick and stubby cock springing forth even as she fisted one of her hands. She'd make him hurt so badly he wouldn't want sex for a month.

Her mouth curled. Sharlene would probably be singing her praises, if she only knew.

Calvin looked down. "That's it, whore," he said thickly, "take me in your mouth and suck hard."

In his dreams.

"Calvin! Oh. My. God."

Brandy dropped her fisted hand as Calvin stumbled back, giving her a clear view of a flame-faced Sharlene...and a white-faced Blaine.

She swallowed. Always inscrutable, this once Blaine looked barely controlled. But of course. He'd paid an obscene amount to be with her tonight. Seeing her apparently servicing someone else was the worst kind of business practice from someone in her profession.

Her eyes met Blaine's. "It's not what it looks like..."

She clamped her mouth shut. Even to her own ears her words sounded lame. She glanced at Calvin, who was busy fumbling with his trousers. For the first time as a call girl, she felt ashamed. A whore on her knees with a man's trousers around his feet.

No one would believe she hadn't wanted this as much as Sharlene's husband.

She pushed back a wave of crushing defeat. She'd never once allowed herself to feel dirty in her chosen career, until now. Somehow she kept her shudders all on the inside. Dear god, she'd never felt more soiled.

Sex was her trade of choice. But not like this...never like this.

Blaine had always treated her as a successful businesswoman and a princess rolled into one. He'd at least give her a chance. "Blaine, you believe me, don't you?"

A muscle in his jaw jerked. His eyes glinted with raw betrayal.

Funny the ache inside her chest, knowing his mistrust really did mean the end of their business dealings. No second chances, no going back. Though she'd had full intention of terminating their arrangement, deep down she'd hoped it wasn't the end. Not really.

The world's stupidest call girl. Who'd have thought?

Sharlene's eyes flashed. Evidently stunned into silence at what she'd witnessed, she became vocal with her accusations as she faced her. "You couldn't bloody wait to pay me back, could you?" she spat. "After all those years of me being better than you, this was your perfect revenge." A tear trekked its way down her makeup-caked face. "Well, I hope you're satisfied."

Brandy rocked back onto her knees. "Your husband followed me in here."

Calvin snorted. "You wanted my money, you greedy little slut. You seduced me! Why else would you have used these restrooms?" He turned to his wife. "You know this doesn't mean anything to me, sweetheart."

Brandy knew there was little point in defending herself, and she cared less what they believed about her anyway. Blaine was the only one whose faith and trust she wanted. Needed. Shame she couldn't even have that.

She gathered up her clutch purse and its scattered belongings as a numbness took hold within. Only when Blaine's warm hand enclosed one of hers did any sense of feeling return. She looked up at his serious, set face as he hauled her effortlessly to her feet.

"I'm taking you home." His hand remained curled around hers when he turned to Calvin and said in a tone of voice that dared rebuke, "You ever call my woman a slut or whore again, and I will destroy you."

Her head whirled. *My woman?* He did believe her then?

Blaine's arm around her waist secured her to his side when they left a stuttering Calvin behind with his enraged wife. She looked up at her savior as they headed toward the exit, but his face was unreadable, even when he nodded to a couple of guests who'd drifted away from the fundraiser, the same as themselves.

The band was breaking into Roy Orbison's lively, upbeat theme song from *Pretty Woman* when they walked out the exit doors. The sheer coincidence might have been amusing under different circumstances.

Once in his Porsche and on the road, it soon became apparent they weren't heading to his townhouse. She turned to him. "Where are we going?"

His profile looked stark beneath the intermittent flashes of streetlights. "Home. Like I said."

Oh? She knew he owned plenty of other houses in other countries around the world, but hadn't realized he owned another in this city.

When he pulled into the driveway of a huge, sprawling harbor-side mansion, she peered at him once again. But he kept silent, brooding, even when he climbed out and opened her passenger door to escort her inside.

Her heels tapped on the hardwood floors, echoing in the cavernous room that appeared to be all stainless steel fixtures and huge, dark-tinted windows. Red sofas and an eight-seat table with red candlesticks as its centerpiece were bright splashes of color against the stark white walls of an open lounge and dining room.

It appeared his passionate streak was spreading further than the bedroom.

"Impressive," she voiced aloud, striving for a normalcy she didn't feel. She turned to him, but he was already behind her, dominant and oh so tall. "And it's yours?" she asked.

"Ours."

"Ours?" she repeated weakly.

Surely he didn't want her as his mistress now? At least, not after what he thought he saw between her and Calvin. And surely he didn't for one moment imagine she wanted to become exclusive?

Yet, despite inner denial, a yearning built and built, overwhelming and all too needy.

"Yours and mine," he said almost savagely, his words slicing through the air as though they were ready to inflict harm.

Her eyes narrowed. Whatever Blaine had kept from her on the journey here, it was all too apparent now. He was a man wounded and bristling with emotions longing to get out. An explosion just waiting to happen.

Her sigh was all on the inside, right along with the heartache. He hadn't believed her innocence then. What had she expected? When it came down to it, she was nothing more than his paid fuck. She'd do well to remember it.

She died a little inside, even before she pulled out a foil from her clutch bag and placed it into his hand. She couldn't face his accusations. Not now, when things were still so raw. Maybe not ever. No, she knew better ways for him to blow off some steam. When she pivoted from him, she blinked back tears before tossing her bag onto the sofa and heading toward the lounge room's balcony doors.

Far-off music from a late-night party trickled inside as she stepped out onto the terrace and slowly peeled off her dress, her movements on autopilot.

The cool touch of night air caressed her breasts, which were still aching and sore from Calvin's unwanted attentions. She pressed a hand to her mouth and beat down the revolting memory, right along with the knowledge of Blaine's low opinion of her.

She'd dwell on all the hurt later. Right now, Blaine was a client, first and foremost.

Right now, she needed to forget.

# Chapter Twelve

She sensed Blaine behind her seconds before he spoke. "We don't have to do this," he said. "Not now."

She didn't turn around. "But I do," she whispered. "I really do."

She only hoped Blaine would understand. She'd lived a good part of her life needing sex to make things right in her world. She had no doubt the moment he took her in his arms that Calvin's name would be diluted, right along with Blaine's distrust...and all the rest of the bad stuff in her life.

His big hands were suddenly on her shoulders, moving up and down her arms before his mouth gently nuzzled her throat. She relaxed against him, his deft touch creating a magic within that she could never quite define.

No one triggered all the right buttons as he did. No one else affected her in every way that counted.

She released a pent-up sigh. It wasn't sex she needed. It was Blaine.

One of his hands touched her evidently bruised upper arm. She flinched and his hands stilled, his voice low. "Much as I do want you right now, maybe it's not such a good idea."

She closed her eyes, willing back composure. Jesus. She was a call girl, men paid to have sex with her. She wasn't going to let the bruise of one bad incident ruin her reputation—ruin it for her clients and for herself. And she most certainly wasn't going to let Blaine think she didn't want him.

She needed to lose herself with him. Needed her arms around his neck and her legs around his hips.

His hands dropped. "At least not this soon after—"

"Right now is perfect," she interrupted with a quick, throaty laugh. She arched against him. "I love sex, you know that."

Blaine's arousal kicked against her even as a profanity seemed wrenched from the depths of his soul. His hands lifted and her breath hitched as he cupped her breasts. She barely repressed a moan as pain arced through the inflamed nerve endings.

He stilled once again, though his voice was thick with lust. "Are you sure you're into this tonight?"

She took his hands in hers and dragged them downward, away from her tender breasts and toward the moist entrance between her thighs. "You even need to ask?"

His long exhalation was hot on her throat. "Then don't move."

His jacket rustled, then his shirt. His belt slid free before the unmistakable sound of a zipper came undone. She shivered, reminded again, all too glaringly, of the fate she'd only just escaped at Calvin's hands.

She heard the tearing of the foil she'd given him. She swallowed back sudden grief. Had he decided she'd proven herself too untrustworthy now *not* to use protection? It took only seconds for him to roll on the condom before he was close behind her again. And despite her ragged emotions, it was as if his big body shielded hers from all that was bad in the world.

"In all my life, I've never wanted any woman half as much as you," he said hoarsely.

Something within her chest shifted, even as any lingering reservations melted clean away. Blaine would never hurt her. Not deliberately. He'd worship her if she let him. When his mouth closed over one side of her throat again and he gently suckled, she completely surrendered to him, to the moment.

Blaine really would make her forget the bad memories by creating some new.

He used gentle hands to slip inside the front of her miniscule thong and massage her clit, deft strokes that slowly escalated in pressure until she moaned, on the verge of convulsing with orgasm.

She could have sobbed when he removed his hand.

"Not yet, baby." Taking hold of her thong, he jerked the satin and lace apart. As it fell to the floor, he growled approvingly, "Much better. Now bend over for me and hold onto the railing."

Throat dry and pulse racing, she did as he requested, the rail cool under her suddenly damp palms.

"So beautiful," he muttered thickly from behind as he guided his cock into the waiting folds of her pussy. She caught her breath at the exquisite pressure that bordered between pleasure and pain, aware that the remnants of anxiety had tossed her emotions around and caused her muscles to clench a little tighter around him.

He pushed his cock to the hilt with a groan. She stifled a whimper that was stark desire. She needed this, needed him, so much. She jerked her hips forward, partly unsheathing his cock. She thrust back, his cock refilling her pussy and his growl filling the air. His hands settled on her hips before he began stroking in and out with alternating long and short slides.

She counterthrusted against him even as she bit back a sob. Deep down, she sensed she'd lost a little piece of herself the moment Calvin had caused this man to doubt her integrity. But knowing this was their last night together...god, she wanted Blaine with an even greater need than before, an elemental yearning she couldn't fight.

"Don't hold back on me, baby," Blaine said hoarsely, "I don't want to climax without you."

Her heart lurched. Tears welled. He wanted to share the magic between them—because that was what it was, magic. And somehow, that knowledge alone drove away the shadows, the old insecurities. She met him stroke for stroke, craving the release that was already blurring everything into insignificance.

With their flesh slapping and pounding, their groans and grunts intermingling, she was abruptly pitched headlong into a climax that took away all breath. All doubt. She soared and peaked, then slowly drifted back to earth.

Blaine climaxed right after, her name falling from his lips, his breath shuddering right along with his body. He sagged against her and pulled her closer still, keeping her that way long after their pulses had slowed and their breaths had softened.

Music continued to waft over them when he finally disconnected from her and disposed of the condom. When he returned and tangled his fingers through hers, she couldn't help but experience a sense of rightness.

A sense of belonging.

She quashed the sentiment. But as he led her back through the lounge and dining room before taking a huge staircase to the next floor, her legs were unforgivably shaky.

In what had to be the master bedroom, he pushed her gently onto a king-size bed and followed her down, his cock hardening against her belly. His mouth covered hers as he kissed her with nothing short of a skill that left her hungry for more.

This was what she loved. This was who she was.

Never again would she allow someone to take that away from her.

His tongue pushed between the seam of her lips, tasting within. One of his hands slid between her thighs, one finger, then two, delving deep inside, exploring the wet inner tissue.

*Oh god.*

Passion stirred and quickly built. Blaine was an amazing and accomplished lover. She knew from past experience that he could easily go two or three rounds in one night.

She'd never once complained about his prowess—until his chest mashed against her breasts. At her sudden sharp inhalation, he reared back. Even in the shadowed room, she could make out the flash of concern in his eyes.

"Kate?"

*I can never be Kate to you.*

She swallowed back a sob and pressed splayed hands onto his chest, pushing him onto his back and climbing aboard. Distracting him before he asked any more questions. He'd already presumed her guilt. She failed to see a need to prove otherwise now. Besides, he'd only see her dim outline, not her bruised flesh.

Kneeling high, she clamped hold of the base of his cock and lowered herself onto his hard length, inch by glorious inch. It wasn't until she began to rock slowly up and down that she acknowledged her oversight.

She released an unsteady breath. "We didn't use a condom."

Blaine moaned, "I know."

She stilled on the upstroke. "You don't care?"

"It's hardly the first time."

So he didn't think her untrustworthy?

"If you accept my offer, there'll never be a need for condoms again."

His hands lifted, fingertips gliding ever so gently yet skillfully around her breasts. After Calvin's brutal touch, Blaine's tenderness there was almost her undoing.

"Don't," she said instead, her voice a sandpaper rasp when desire and anguish for what might have been hit in equal measure.

His hands dropped. He clasped her hips, dragging her down on his shaft before urging her back up again, creating an almost choreographed rhythm. "Don't think I don't care about what almost happened between you and Calvin, because I do—I really do."

She froze, though every atom in her body screamed that she grind her pussy, her clit, against his cock.

"Something inside me snapped when I saw you with him," he said starkly. "Everything I'd planned..."

"Planned?" she croaked.

His hands balled into fists. "Never mind," he uttered raggedly. "Just know that if I can't have you any other way, I'm willing to pay whatever necessary to make you stay."

His words were a slap to her face. Yes, her body paid the bills, but she wasn't without a soul.

She pulled free from him and stood beside the bed.

His breath rushed out before he reached over and flicked on a bedside lamp.

She scarcely noticed. Her voice shook. "Call girls have standards too. I'm proud of my chosen profession and have never lied about who I am and what I do."

"What. The. Fuck."

She frowned at his words, and the way his sharp stare focused on her breasts, before taking in her upper arm.

*Oh shit.*

She glanced down. One of her breasts was discolored by a mottled purple-blue bruise, the other looking only slightly less painful. Her upper arm revealed obvious finger imprints.

His stare caught hers. His face was drawn into even harder angles and planes. "Calvin?"

She nodded. "Yeah."

"My god. You should have said something—"

Anger surged. "I tried, remember? But you didn't believe me." She swung away as tears welled and hurt clutched at her soul.

"Where are you going?" he gritted.

She cast him one last, lingering look, even as defeat scored her words. "Home. My home."

"Kate. Don't leave, not like this. Please..."

"It's over, Blaine." She held on to her poise, her willpower, with everything she had. "Consider our last night together a freebie."

# Chapter Thirteen

Kate spooned another mouthful of silky-smooth chocolate ice cream between her lips. Her favorite comfort food slid down her throat on a gusty sigh, causing a little blob to land on her old t-shirt.

She shrugged. For once, there was no one to impress.

It's why she enjoyed nothing better than wandering around her apartment in old sweats and an even older tee, makeup-less and hair left to its own devices. Add reruns of *Friends* on her plasma TV, and she was one happy woman.

Except she wasn't happy, not by a long shot.

No overindulgence could offset the brittle emptiness within. No other man could possibly take the place of the one man she really wanted.

When she'd told the agency she was taking a week off, they'd been far from happy.

Too bad.

She needed time alone. Time to think. Time to sort out all the thoughts and uncertainties tangled in her mind. A week of overeating, moping and generally not giving a stuff about anything at all.

But day one of her self-imposed solitude and she already missed Blaine, as if she'd been his sweetheart, the love of his life, instead of his whore.

*Fucking idiot.*

She pushed another mouthful of ice cream into her gob at about the same time the doorbell buzzed. Placing her half-full bowl on the coffee table, she checked the peephole before unlocking and opening the door to a flower delivery man.

"Kate Matthews?" the gray-bearded, Santa-lookalike asked.

"Yes."

Who would send flowers to Kate and not Brandy? The agency forwarded gifts from clients on a regular basis, but none knew her real name or where she lived.

Except for Blaine. Well, he knew her name, she could bet he probably knew where she lived too.

She accepted the proffered bunch of crimson roses with little pockets of baby's breath. Absently thanking the delivery man before he marched away, she closed her eyes to breathe in the sweet, old-fashioned rose scent.

"The color made me think of you."

Her eyes popped open, dismay and stark need fighting for dominance as her stare connected to Blaine's. She might have surmised the flowers were from him, but she never imagined he'd be part of the package.

He appeared indolent and at ease propped against the far wall near the twin elevators. His tall, masculine figure in jeans and a white tee looked even more arresting. But she knew he was anything but relaxed.

Right now, she could well imagine him born on the wrong side of the tracks. He was brooding and dangerous. And way too disturbing for her peace of mind.

"How did you know?" she whispered.

He raised a brow, though his stare was steely hard with intent. "That you'd be home all this week or your address?" At her shocked hiss of breath, he said unapologetically, "A man of my means has ways."

So someone from the agency had chosen money over discretion? No, that'd be a breach of contract. He'd obviously hired a private investigator.

She withdrew from the doorway, shoulders shaking with barely suppressed anger at his arrogance. He'd really crossed a line this time. "You should have respected my privacy."

In a couple of strides, he was in front of her, a hand on the door to keep it open. "And I should have trusted you." He released a long, slow breath. "Kate, I'm sorry I misjudged you, sorry for not believing in you." He raked a hand through his hair. "I should have listened to you long before I forced Calvin to tell me the truth."

A picture of a blubbering, wrecked Calvin filled her head. The self-important, son of a bitch wouldn't have broken easily.

"I let you down. But believe me when I say Calvin won't dare bother you or anyone again."

She released a heavy breath and nodded. "I'm glad." She didn't want the details. Calvin deserved whatever Blaine gave him. And then some.

His face was shadowed, pained. "And I won't ever presume you're safe away from me again."

She shook her head, aware more than ever that now was the time to assert herself. "You were my client. Nothing more. It's not your place to worry."

"Is that really all I was to you?" he asked softly.

She refrained from screaming out the denial that was lodged like acid at the base of her throat. Instead she let out a sigh and said, "I looked good on your arm. End of story. I'm not made of glass. I can look after myself."

If hurt showed before, he barely held anger in check as he asked, "When are you going to let yourself trust someone, Kate?" He shoved a hand through his hair. "Or is sex the only time you let down your guard and lose your inhibitions?"

She gasped, her hand lifting of its own volition and delivering a stinging slap to his face. "Bastard," she hissed, almost physically sick from the emotions churning in her belly. Not helped one bit by striking out at the man forcing her to admit the truth. Yet somehow she couldn't plug the resentment within. "And my name's Brandy. It will always be Brandy to you."

She stepped back and put pressure on the door to swing it shut.

His expression hardened. He blocked the door with a foot. "No, Kate. I'm sorry, but I can't accept that."

The lump in her belly grew. "You don't have a choice," she said, but there was too little conviction in her voice.

"We all have choices. Let me in," he said. "Please. Give me at least a couple of minutes to plead my case."

Kate swallowed. Shit. She really shouldn't. This was mad, stupid. But the sincerity in his usually intense expression couldn't be denied. She swung open the door. She'd give him a chance to explain himself and then he'd be gone from her life.

Permanently this time.

The queasiness in her belly returned tenfold.

She nodded. "Fine. Two minutes. No more."

It sounded final. Absolute. Such scant time to drink in his every nuance of expression before she shut the door on him for good.

If he had similar thoughts, he didn't show it. Quite the contrary. He strode inside with an assurance that made her chic apartment suddenly stifling in a hot, cramped kind of way. And this time she couldn't blame her swirling belly.

He turned to her. "Kate, I don't want to lose you."

On unsteady legs she walked to her quaint little bar with its handful of quality bottled spirits She needed a drink. Definitely not brandy. Her hands shook more than a little when she poured them both a shot of aged scotch. She handed him a glass, careful not to touch him.

Even one brush of his fingers against hers and she just might not have the willpower to deny him.

She took a sip. "I was only yours for the short time you paid for me, you know that."

He blew out a ragged breath. "As far as I was concerned, you were mine from the first moment I saw you. I never told you this, but I knew of you long before we officially met."

"You did?"

He tossed back the amber liquid, draining it in one long swallow. "You were at a function with a senator at the time."

Her eyes widened. She'd been young and so very green at the time. The senator had been bald, paunchy and twenty years her senior. He'd also been an above-average lover. Shame their last night together had been the night before he'd made his marriage vows to some upper-class matron.

Not that Brandy had known at the time. She'd read about the senator's nuptials in the society pages of the local newspaper the next day. It seemed she'd been his last fling before he'd settled down into a long life of domestic bliss.

Though she'd felt nothing beyond affection for the senator, she could recall even now the twinge of envy knowing she'd been cast aside for someone more acceptable. In that moment, she'd reverted to the little girl whose father had walked out to be with someone else. In that moment, she'd understood a little of her mother's torment.

Despite the senator's obvious lust for her, being unwanted in the one way that counted most had hit her hard.

Pushing aside the unwanted memories, she said at last, "You rang the agency. You must have known my vocation?"

He nodded. "Yes, eventually." He placed his empty glass onto the bar with a clank. "I asked some questions. But no one knew anything about you."

"You hired a detective?"

He grinned. "Nothing that dramatic...at least not back then. I was invited to the senator's wedding. When he went into the men's room I followed him. If I recall correctly, it was at the trough when I asked him about you."

The trough.

Despite herself, a grin pulled at her lips at the wholly unromantic picture. She could well imagine the senator would have felt inadequate beside Blaine. In every way. "What did he say?"

"He gave me your working name and your agency's number before he wished me the best of luck. He understood my obsession."

"But we hadn't even met."

He shrugged his shoulders, a wry smile curling his lips. "What can I say? You caught my attention. I wanted you."

"And you had me." No mention of love at first sight. She bit into her bottom lip. She was such a fool to even allow the idea to cross her mind. How many times did she have to remind herself that Blaine wanted her body, nothing else? "But whatever you imagined we shared, it's over now."

He rubbed a hand over a jaw darkened by stubble. A casual gesture, but his eyes were lit with determination. "Is that what you want?"

She swallowed. Could he read her inner doubts?

"I know a little of your past," he said gently. "Know you were bullied by your peers."

Realization hit. "Oh my god. Is that what the fundraiser was all about?" she whispered.

His nostrils flared, as though he was a stallion ready to fight and defend. "Yes."

So it hadn't just been about his own past bullying that had prompted him to support the fundraiser. Despite his obvious probing into her past, she couldn't help but feel touched. What he'd done went beyond anything she could have imagined in her wildest dreams. In trying to heal some of her hurt, he'd helped countless others, too.

He lifted a hand. "If that means helping you face your past, then I've achieved my goal."

"Why?" she asked. "Why would you do that for me?"

He stepped toward her, his face stark with need. "Don't you understand?" he asked softly. "I'm here to stay. God, Kate. Not everyone in your life wants to walk away."

Her mouth dried and pain hit, sharp and intense. Surely he couldn't know that her father had left her mother for a younger woman? Surely he couldn't know her deepest fear was that same scenario happening all over again?

It would break her if she accepted his offer, only to watch him walk away from her. But even worse would be his staying long term out of a sense of guilt. She sucked in a steadying breath. Despite all that, she wanted to tell him a little about her family, needed to get some issues off her chest. If there was anyone she could trust enough to tell, it was Blaine.

"Yeah. Good old Dad walked out on my mom and me just months after a gas stove explosion left terrible scarring on her face." She shook her head with slow, remembered pain. "Gives you great faith in humanity, doesn't it?"

Shit. Where had those words come from?

Blaine's hands on her shoulders warmed her. His face was all compassionate understanding. "You've been conditioned into believing looks are everything. Kate, you *are* beautiful. Inside and out. Hell, you're perfect to me right now, with your hair mussed and wearing an old t-shirt."

She looked up at him and released a little sigh, wishing she could believe him. Every time she looked in the mirror, she hoped her reflection didn't reveal someone horrid. "I'm happy enough with my life now."

"Really?" He looked toward the puddle of melted ice cream in her bowl. "So why the comfort food?"

She frowned, and then stepped back. His hands dropped from her shoulders at about the same time her defenses came up, like steel gates keeping out an unwanted visitor. "I enjoy junk food."

"As a teenager, probably yes. As an adult, I'm betting you prefer the gym and retail therapy."

Holy crap. What didn't he know about her? She glared. "Your two minutes are up."

His stare held hers, seemingly searching for answers. He expelled a rough breath before he nodded and said quietly, "I'll wait for you, baby."

She stood unmoving, her heart aching while he let himself out of the apartment, taking away all that was good in her world. Only long after he was gone and she'd finally shut the door did she realize that yes, maybe he would wait for her. But how long would he stay if she accepted his offer? How long before he walked out on her too, just like her dad?

# Chapter Fourteen

Kate spent the rest of the week vacillating between needing Blaine with a quiet desperation that left her inwardly reeling, and a contrary desire to escape the man causing the tumultuous emotions.

Even putting on a brave face in front of her trio of friends hadn't stopped them from asking concerned questions and treating her like spun glass. It was as if all the attention had swung from Claire to Kate. Being surrounded by their sympathetic looks and compassionate understanding had only made her feel ten times worse.

She didn't want to be reminded of the wreck her life had become. She wanted everything back to normal again.

By the end of the week, she knew she had to get back on the wagon, so to speak, back into a routine. She'd come to accept that Blaine had never been part of her future plans, at least not long term, just the same way she wasn't part of his long-term future.

It was in his DNA to want what he couldn't have. She'd made a living on that logic alone. She also knew he'd get tired of waiting and come after her, and claim what he thought was his.

At least short term.

It was past time to move on.

The sooner she left, the sooner Blaine would forget about her and find someone else unattainable. Or maybe he'd meet someone perfect for him in every way. Wife and potential mother-to-his-children material.

She closed her eyes for a moment as pain washed over her anew. She had to get through this, had to forget about Blaine. And if the only way to do that was to leave the country for a couple of weeks, then so be it.

She opened her eyes on a shuddering breath before she snapped shut her carry-on luggage.

Everything was in place. She'd accepted an Italian count's proposal to stay with him for a few weeks in his luxury five-star hotel. Count Pierre Moretti had been a regular john once, before she'd minimized her lovers.

He'd been generous, if a little sleazy.

She inwardly shrugged. Perhaps this time she'd give in to his request that she fuck another woman while he watched. At least it might take her mind off of a certain male for a while.

*Yeah, fat chance.*

Her cell buzzed. She frowned. Caller ID showed a private number. And no one who knew her business number rang her incognito.

It had to be Blaine.

She wouldn't answer.

No way.

*Fuck it.*

"Brandy," she said huskily.

"Kate. I thought I could leave you alone. I can't."

"Blaine, don't," she whispered, voice cracking. "Just...don't."

For the sake of her weakening resolve.

"I'm coming over."

"No. I won't be here. I'm...leaving. You won't see me again."

"Kate, no!"

"Goodbye, Blaine."

"Don't hang up—"

As she disconnected, she couldn't stop the sudden flood of tears from falling down her face, couldn't keep all the discordant emotions from spilling free.

She looked around her apartment. She'd lived a good life here, and made some great friends. But maybe it was time to start fresh...with everything. She would hire a discreet moving company to pack away her possessions and put them into storage. Then she'd sell this place.

And then?

It didn't really matter. She'd nurse her bruised heart and rebuild her life, in just the same way she had after her parents' breakup.

Her mother's suicide.

She sucked in a breath, striving not to open the floodgates to the memories that were so painful, she never revisited. But suddenly the recollection hit her front and center, and she was a spectator looking in from the outside.

Kate stopped at the wire gate that hung crookedly from its hinges, admirably showcasing the neglect of the front yard. Not to mention the home and the people within it.

She scuffed her worn sneaker on the cracked sidewalk, beyond reluctant to enter the house that had long ago stopped being a home.

In the three months since her dad had walked out on them, her once vivacious mother had become as scarred on the inside as she was on the outside. A listless, uncaring woman whose inner torment pushed away her only child...who wanted nothing more than to love her.

She sighed, wishing she could simply turn away and leave, run away from the life that'd somehow befallen her.

*Leave? And go where? Back to school where the vultures want to pick off what is left of my pride?*

The only thing she had to look forward to at school was Jeremy, the boy two years her senior. He'd been sending her secretive smiles and suggestive glances for weeks now. Oh, she knew he wanted one thing and one thing only—he'd already been with at least a handful of girls in his class—but the thrill and flattery of it all outweighed any of the negative.

She was wanted. And that counted for more than just about anything in her life right now.

Another sigh left her lips, a far more wretched sound than before, as she walked up the short, weed-infested path to the front door. Time to clean the mess that was undoubtedly inside. Time to cook and play slave in waiting to her shell of a mother. The same mother whose selfish need to vent on her daughter had worn Kate down until she wondered if this life was the only one she deserved.

She opened the front door with dread.

Her eyes widened. Awareness hit her hard. In the tiny entrance hallway, the gold-framed mirror that'd once hung in pride of place had been knocked to the floor, big, jagged pieces of glass littering the faded tan carpet.

"Mother!"

Her breath caught. Her pulse thundered in her ears. Everything within her knew something was horribly wrong.

She sprinted into the sparse, open kitchen and dining room. Her eyes jerked left and right. The squeaky clean interior frightened her as much as the broken mirror in the entryway.

Perhaps more.

"Mother!" she screamed.

The two bedrooms of the house were empty. Shit. Where was she? Kate pressed a hand to her mouth. Had her mother left her, too?

No, impossible. Her mother had become all but housebound, detesting the burns that caused people to give her long, pitying looks...the same burns that had caused her husband to leave her for someone else. Someone young and pretty. Someone without any scars.

Kate only saw the wounds on her mother's inside now. A disfigurement that'd been left by a callous, cold-hearted husband who'd decided a beautiful girlfriend was more important than loving his wife, his family.

If she hated her mother, then she sincerely loathed her father. He'd deserted them when they'd needed him most and left behind a toxic wasteland Kate had no idea how to fix.

A dripping tap abruptly snared her attention. She froze. The repetitive sound was loud as a drum in the stifling silence.

The bathroom.

She crashed open its door.

Her mother's body lay lifeless in the tub. Blood-red water overflowed the rim and onto the white-tiled floor. A hand still clutched a jagged piece of broken glass she'd used to slit her wrists.

"Mom," she whispered numbly.

# Chapter Fifteen

Paris. A city of love and romance.

Brandy could only hope a little of that would rub off on her and lend her...something. Anything. Because right now, she felt little more than dull apathy.

She brushed at her arms as a chill settled over her. She was turning into her mother. A shell with too little life and light left inside.

Except, unlike her mother, at least she still had her looks.

*And when those looks fade...?*

She gnawed at her bottom lip, her hands interlacing. She'd worry about that when it happened. For now, she was youthful and beautiful and should be enjoying every moment of it.

Besides, she'd have made her money by then. When her call girl days were behind her, she'd be wealthy in her own right.

She sagged against the luxurious leather seat, taking deep, calming breaths. This was the life she'd fought hard to attain. This was the life she'd always wanted. Except people grew and changed. Some even discovered that what they'd once wanted badly and finally got was no longer of consequence.

Had that happened to her?

Financial ease. Men adoring her. Independence.

Shouldn't that be enough?

But something within her *had* changed. She couldn't deny it any longer. The incredible wonder she'd experienced from her very first sexual encounter, and then all the ones afterward, had faded. She wanted only to recall and embrace that heady feeling again.

She closed her eyes, thinking back to the day that'd changed her whole life, and sent her into the call girl profession.

ॐ

"Where do you think you're going, young lady?"

Kate paused, hating the tone of condescension in her foster dad's voice. Even without seeing him from where he sat behind the horrid floral couch, she could well imagine the contempt pressed into his haughty face. "Out."

Was it wrong to hate her foster parents? After all, they'd taken her in after her mother's death, clothed and fed her. But the one thing she craved—love—they'd been unable to give her.

The feeling was mutual.

She snorted. The pair of them barely loved one another. How did she expect them to embrace her too?

"Not a good idea," her foster mum chimed in from beside her husband on the couch. "The last thing you need is to have some fella take advantage of you and knock you up."

"That's not going to happen—"

"Leaving you with some bastard child," her foster mother continued, "just like what happened to your mother with you."

Kate strode over to the front of the couch and faced her revolting foster parents with nothing less than scorn. "I'd rather live my life the way my mother did, loving someone wholeheartedly, than end my days as a loveless sack of shit like you two."

She turned away with them both shouting obscenities. She didn't care. She wouldn't be going back. Not for anything. From now on, she'd make her own way in the world.

Somehow.

The moon was a tiny sliver high in the sky, barely yielding any light. But never had the night looked more beautiful, dark velvet edged with untold promise. She all but skipped to the car waiting just down the road from her house.

And as she climbed into the front seat, she didn't think beyond the moment when Jeremy, no longer a school student but an apprentice in his father's law firm, dragged her toward him in the driver's seat and kissed her like he couldn't get enough.

Seventeen and never been kissed, Kate responded to him equally as passionately...

꙳

Brandy smiled as the car braked to a stop and the memory faded.

She'd lost her inhibitions all those years ago. Jeremy had made the girl a woman. And then, when he'd been about to drive her home and she explained she had no home to go to anymore, he'd inadvertently turned her into a businesswoman.

He'd given her a hundred-dollar note and planted the seed that would become her future inside her head.

She often wondered what her life would have been like had her father taken her into his new life. But she hadn't been wanted, not by him or his new girlfriend. They hadn't wanted her to hinder their newfound romance.

Looking back, she sensed her dad had been unable to face the guilt, hadn't wanted to appease his daughter's raw despair and disgust.

A valet opened her door. She nodded thanks, pushing all the negative thoughts aside even as her heels clacked on the pebbled drive of the hotel's grand portico entrance. Leaving her luggage in the capable hands of the hotel's porters, she approached the Count, who waited for her beside the huge glass doors.

Though nothing like Blaine, Pierre was nevertheless charming and good-looking in his own way, with his olive skin and messily styled, raven-colored hair.

"Thank you for coming," he said with a wide smile, his appreciative gaze sliding over her as though he was a bidder at auction eyeing a fine filly. "I trust you had an enjoyable flight?"

She accepted his outstretched hands with a gracious smile and murmured, "I did. Your private jet is opulent and beyond comfortable."

"Good, good." He brought her in close before one of his arms snaked around her waist.

She leaned into him, though every instinct screamed at her to step away. His touch on her felt wrong.

"Come." He drew her inside the huge entrance doors. A waterfall cascaded over rocks the size of boulders between the escalators. Huge chandeliers glittered from a high-domed ceiling. "Let me show you around before we get down to business."

She nodded stiffly before casting him the most enticing expression she could muster. "Sure."

Somehow the coming seduction held no appeal. She should blame Calvin for that. But she knew without a doubt, it was Blaine who'd compromised her enjoyment and passion of being with anyone else. She'd be unable to help comparing her clients to him. Their touches, their glances. God, their everything would all be sadly lacking.

*I'm in love with Blaine.*

Realization hit and left her reeling. But then a smile lit her face and she realized she was anything but stricken. It certainty made things a whole lot easier to deal with. No more indecision. No more being too scared to face the truth.

She'd tell the Count her true feelings and hope he had enough romance within him to understand.

But then he swept her into a melee of people and noise, and she knew she'd have to leave blurting out her confession until a little later.

Blaine strode through the expansive lobby of the lavish hotel, his eyes taking in little else but the guests milling around.

His gut clenched with an urgency borne of desperation as he scanned and disregarded every woman in the vicinity. None had Kate's glorious strawberry-blonde hair. None had her gorgeous svelte figure along with an aura, a presence, that drew the eye.

The sick feeling in the pit of his belly grew and grew.

*Fuck.* He was too late. Way too late.

He could picture, all too clearly, Kate—his Kate—beneath the Count, her eyes closed in ecstasy with her lips plundered and her body strummed as if it was some well-loved instrument.

His jaw clenched, teeth aching with the effort to restrain the anger within. Pierre Moretti wasn't the right man for Kate. Christ, the man didn't love her. He had no right to touch her, kiss her and fuck her.

None.

It mattered little to him that Kate's profession gave the man every right in the world to touch, kiss and fuck her.

She. Was. His.

He drew in a long, steadying breath. He'd hoped the week she'd taken off on her own volition would make her see what he knew she felt, if only she'd admit it.

She loved him as much as he loved her.

But it seemed it'd had the reverse effect. And little wonder. He'd turned his back on her when she'd needed him most. He'd presumed the worst of her, believed the sack of shit, Calvin, over her. By doing so he'd rejected the goodness she carried inside her like a torch, the same goodness that'd attracted him to her right from the start.

Though few people saw the vulnerability beneath her worldly outer shell, he'd always seen it. He'd had no excuse to throw her vulnerability right back in her face. He could only guess that by doing so, her battered emotions had pushed her right back into the ingrained habits she'd spent half a lifetime grooming, probably from the day she lost her virginity.

But did she really think those habits would stave off whatever demons she carried around from her past?

He'd had the rest of her history thoroughly investigated in the week she'd taken off work…in the week he'd gone out of his mind with wanting her. At least now, everything about her made sense. Aside from the fact that she loved sex, it was little wonder she'd fallen into the role of call girl.

She faced abandonment issues few people could understand. First, her father walked away from his family, and then her mother took her own life. On top of it all, she'd had a childhood of bullying to contend with. Little wonder she didn't trust easily. Didn't love easily.

As a call girl, she was in control of the situation…the man. She was the one who walked away—always. She was the beautiful woman clients didn't want to lose, not the other way around.

A flash of red caught his eye, startling him out of his reverie.

Kate. And her client.

The Count, a renowned playboy and party animal, snagged her close as they stopped at a bank of elevators. Blaine's heartbeat quickened. The surroundings dimmed, his focus all on Kate. She looked beautiful, elegant and sexy. But he knew her well enough to see she hid her true feelings. She was every bit as wretched as he was right now.

His limbs moved before he'd even formulated a plan.

There was no time for thinking. Only action.

"Kate!"

Brandy stiffened, causing her client's arm to tighten around her.

Blaine?

No. Impossible.

The elevator doors glided apart. She stepped inside the carriage with Pierre, determination filling her. Finally alone, she could tell the man who was supposed to be her client the truth.

Then she heard a much louder and more desperate shout.

"Kate, stop!"

"Someone's got it bad," chuckled the Count, his arm once again tightening around her waist. "I wonder who the elusive Kate is?"

Brandy held her breath, fixated by the elevator doors as they silently began to glide shut. At least, until a pair of hands took hold and put a halt to the automatic function.

A total sense of unreality swept over her as the doors held, then re-opened, framing Blaine, who stood outside the elevator. Dizziness assailed her. She shouldn't be surprised. Deep down, she'd known it was him the moment he'd called out her name.

A muscle jumped in Blaine's jaw. "You're wearing red."

She swallowed. Managing a nod, she uttered inanely, "Yes, it's...I'm so used to the color..."

"Kate, don't do this," he said softly, though every atom inside her body perceived he was hurting.

The Count peered down at her, his face perplexed. "Brandy?"

Her attention stayed fixated on Blaine. "I can't be your mistress, Blaine."

What she'd known all along—if she'd only admitted it to herself—struck her like a lightning bolt. Blaine was all or nothing. She couldn't accept him any other way.

He shook his head, as though disbelieving her logic. "That's not what I want either. I only offered you that because that's all you seemed willing to give."

She blinked. Was he for real? Did he seriously want more from her?

"I want all of you, Kate. Not just what you can give me in the bedroom. I want to have a home with you...a family. Everything." He smiled a slightly lopsided smile. "After I'd coerced you into attending the fundraiser, I'd planned to do this whole romantic proposal thing once we were alone—"

Proposal?

Her breath caught in her throat as hope bloomed and spread. "Wh...what?"

A crowd was beginning to gather outside, watching the spectacle unfold.

"I realize now what I should have a long time ago. The most precious things in life can't be bought. Baby, your love is priceless." Blaine dug into his jacket pocket. He sank onto one knee, an opened jewelry box with a gorgeous gold ring encrusted with diamonds sitting snugly inside. "I want a lifetime with you, Kate. As my wife."

Someone in the crowd oohed.

Blaine's attention remained fixed on her. "Will you marry me?"

She was speechless. Stunned. She'd gotten him so wrong! She'd experienced prejudice as a call girl, and yet she'd been so incredibly judgmental herself on so many levels. When he'd shown her the harbor-side mansion, it wasn't because he'd wanted her there as his mistress. She had no doubt in her mind right now that he'd planned to reveal it after he'd proposed.

It was what he'd wanted to talk to her about before his cell had interrupted the conversation. Then she'd left his house before he'd come home.

She squeezed her eyes closed. If only she'd damn well stayed the night, then maybe all the heartache, the misunderstandings and pain could have been avoided.

When he'd told her he was saving the romance for later, he'd really meant it.

She opened her eyes to view his gorgeous face. Her voice cracked. "Yes, Blaine. A million times, yes!"

He grinned, his stare adoring and inconceivably damp. "I love you."

"I love you, too," she whispered, everything inside her overflowing with devotion for the man before her. The man she would marry. The man who'd spent quite some time already on one knee.

He slipped the beautiful ring on her finger. When he straightened, she stepped away from Pierre and into Blaine's arms, only half aware of the smattering of applause and heartfelt sighs outside the elevator.

No more doubts, no more insecurities. She'd love Blaine with everything she had and then some. She *did* love Blaine with everything she had. She looked up at him with tenderness filling her from the inside out. He'd pushed her out of her comfort zone and made her see she wasn't really living, just existing on life's fringes.

Sex couldn't replicate love, no matter how much she enjoyed the act.

Blaine tucked a strand of hair behind her ear, his eyes alight with adoration as he bent his head, and his mouth slanted across hers, sealing the deal. She leaned into him, deepening the kiss, not wanting to ever let him go again.

Someone cleared their throat. Blaine pulled back first, however reluctantly, and glanced at the Count.

The other man shook his head. "And to think I had such grand plans for tonight."

Blaine tucked her closer. She tilted her head up and smiled at her future husband, aware this time his possessiveness felt right. Good.

Blaine dragged his stare from her and back to the other man. "I've already ensured that you'll be compensated for your trouble."

The Count emitted a heavy sigh. "I don't want your money—"

Blaine looked out the elevator doors and jerked his head. Two dark-haired beauties sashayed forward in gold-spangled micro dresses—twins, if Kate wasn't mistaken.

She couldn't stop the peal of laughter bursting free. Only Blaine would make up for the Count's loss, twofold!

"While I know no one else could ever make up for Kate, I didn't want your being alone on my conscience." Blaine nodded to the twins. "Ladies, meet Count Pierre Moretti."

The Count broke into a grin. "Hello, pretty little ladies."

Blaine winked at her, before he took her hand in his. "Let's go home, Kate."

Back to the harbor-side mansion he'd bought for the two of them.

Something shifted inside her chest. Brandy Alexander had been a huge part of her life, but Kate wouldn't be sad to say goodbye to her. No, it was past time she shed her armor and reveled in just being herself.

Plain old Kate Matthews.

Loved and adored by the one man she loved and adored back with all her heart.

It seemed the life she'd once secretly dreamed of having was about to come true after all.

# Epilogue

**K**ate Waymann smiled at Elaine as she accepted the proffered glass of orange juice. Taking a sip, she awkwardly sat back on the red lounge that was positioned next to windows with priceless views of Sydney Harbour.

Though the mansion Blaine had purchased eighteen months previously had cooling breezes from the water, it was an unseasonably hot autumn day, with a storm forecast for later in the day.

Blaine's mother returned her smile. "So how're you feeling, Kate? Not overdoing things, I hope?"

She shook her head, and glanced pointedly at her husband flipping steaks and sausages for lunch out on the balcony barbecue. "Are you kidding me? Blaine is making sure I don't move an inch unless I have to."

Elaine chuckled. "Yeah well, it's not every day a woman is blessed with being pregnant with twins."

Kate put a hand on the swollen basketball shape of her belly. She still had two months until she hit full-term, but the way Blaine coddled her, she'd make it there without any problems. "I know." The room shimmered as she fought back sudden tears. Her damn hormones were turning her into an emotional wreck. "I truly am blessed in every way."

Elaine reached out a hand to cover Kate's. "I'm only glad my son found you. I'm not lying when I say I've never seen him this happy. You're his perfect match in every way."

Kate sniffled and swiped at her eyes. "It means so much to me to hear you say that."

"It's the truth."

Kate's smile wobbled. She was aware that the other woman wasn't just telling her what she wanted to hear. Elaine might be well-mannered and refined, but she was also uncompromising and straight down the line when it came to her son.

When Kate had married Blaine in a small, private ceremony just a week after she'd flown back with him from Paris, his mother had shown her nothing but unreserved love.

"Your part of the Waymann family now." Elaine's eyes glistened, the high emotions of the moment seemingly catching. "The daughter I've always wanted."

Kate swallowed past the lump in her throat. "My past...?"

"Stays in the past where it belongs," the older woman affirmed. She leaned forward, taking Kate's hand in her own. "Sometimes life throws us curve balls and we do what we have to just to survive...even thrive."

Kate stared. Was Elaine hinting that she too had done things that had been morally questionable?

"Is everything okay in here?"

Kate dragged away her consideration of Elaine to look up at Blaine as he strode inside, a tray of cooked meat in hand. Though his query had been controlled, when he glanced at his mother, his eyes revealed undercurrents of disapproval.

Damn, how had she been so lucky to get with a man who loved her unconditionally? A man who'd give her everything he had, and then some, to keep her happy.

"Women's talk, nothing more," Elaine announced before she straightened. "Now let me take that tray to the table for you and I'll get the salad out of the fridge."

When Elaine did just that, her heels retreating into the kitchen, Blaine turned his full attention to Kate. "Baby, seriously, is everything okay?"

Kate sighed, so damn content and in love with her husband it was almost a crime. "Yes, everything's fine." She smiled up at him. "Everything couldn't be more perfect."

The End

*Want more VIP Desire Agency stories by Mel Teshco...*
**High Class**
**Also included in the VIP Desire Agency Boxset**

Claire Davis has done everything possible to give herself and her sisters a simple life since their mother died when she was eighteen. But appearances can be deceiving. She leads a complicated, double life as Scarlet, high class call girl, sleeping with billionaire businessmen to pay the bills. Falling in love has never been part of her plans, especially to a born heart-breaker.

Mackenzie Smitherson has one goal in life: make money, and lots of it. Except the one woman he pays to be with him also turns out to be the one woman whose heart isn't available at any price. He wants more than her beautiful body...he wants all of her. Even if that means he has to open up his heart, and reveal his own dark past. But will Claire walk away to save her own heart before he has a chance?

# Chapter One of High Class

Scarlet moved through the crowded room like she owned it. Tonight she wasn't barely noticeable Claire Davis. Tonight she was a paid seductress on the arm of one of the most famous men in the world.

She smoothed a manicured hand down her simple-but-exclusive white sheath dress, and checked her upswept hair remained in place. And all the while she smiled at the strangers her client, Amos Drynn, lead singer of Frankenstein's Blood, acknowledged with a vague nod of his head.

Many of those strangers were groupies and fans of Frankenstein's Blood. Many of those same fans were also the crème de le crème of the rich and elite, attending this latest good cause.

Tonight's charity auction was as much famed for its items up for bid as it was for its huge fundraising. Tonight Frankenstein's Blood were the main drawcard, and had on offer a one-hour performance for the highest bidder.

With all proceeds going to cancer research, it was a cause that touched her deeply. Her heart ached in an all too familiar way. It'd been a little over six years since her single mother had lost her fight against breast cancer, leaving behind three daughters, two of whom were twins and just barely in their teens.

"Don't look so serious," Amos teased, his muscled, tattooed arm pulling her close. "I don't pay you for that."

She pushed away the ache and arched a fine brow. "I'm also not paid to perform a blow job in front of three hundred people."

His lips curled into a grin, but before he had a chance to reply, a young woman with a pierced brow and nose ring brushed up against him. Her silver-studded thigh-high boots concealed more than her cut-off shorts and sparkly bikini top. "Here's my number," she crooned, pressing a slip of paper into his hands. "Call me anytime."

Amos declined, pushing past the woman of questionable age even as he muttered, "Unfortunately that young lady would do it for free."

Scarlet hid a grimace. She could fully understand why women came onto Amos. Even without his rock star status, he was gorgeous. But it didn't mean she'd join the queue in giving away her sexual expertise.

She had bills to pay, and sisters who relied on her—even more so now that they attended university.

Besides, the rock singer hired her not to service his carnal needs—he had any number of available groupies for that. Scarlet was little more than a professional front, a paid escort Amos wanted only to look pretty on his arm and to conduct half-decent social chitchat.

Unlike Mackenzie Smitherson. She shivered. That man had wanted more than a little from her. He'd taken her all. Again and again. And though he mightn't have tattoos and revealed only a business persona, she'd learned firsthand he didn't hold back in the bedroom.

He was as uninhibited as any wild rock star.

She turned to Amos, smiling at the singer's tough physique and big, inked, biceps. Strangely enough, she was comfortable with him, and liked the fact the bedroom didn't feature in their business transaction. Being with him was like hanging out with a big brother.

He paused, giving her a wink before he tucked a hand behind her head and pressed his lips to hers in a kiss that deliberately lingered.

*Maybe not quite a big brother.*

She leaned into him, going along with the charade that he was taken for the night. She held back a sigh. Although he was a great kisser, there was no spark, no magic in the act.

Not like she'd had with Mackenzie.

*You have to stop thinking about that man!*

She drew back, her face flushed. But not from the kiss ... far from it. Dwelling on Mackenzie and his bedroom skills was enough to send her knees weak and her pulse hammering. And that was despite the fact that after seven years in the sex industry she was becoming jaded.

"Are you okay?" Amos asked, his light blue eyes assessing.

She nodded. He paid her to put on an act, and that was what she'd do. "Never better."

Amos frowned. But before he could question her further, a paunchy, middle-aged man in a suit with a red bow tie approached him. "Sir, the auction is about to start."

Amos nodded and clasped her hand before they followed the older man into the hotel's auditorium. He leaned down and murmured, "Front row seats. Not too shabby."

He took a seat next to his equally famous band members, and she took the one next to him. She leaned her head against his shoulder and he drew an arm around her shoulders.

Her being with him mostly kept the groupies at bay, even as it added to his public persona. It was almost a given that a rock star had a different lover every week. A pity the media had already publicized them being together five times in the last six weeks. It meant their time together was coming to an end.

He'd probably hire another of the girls from the escort agency she worked for. Any one of her agency friends would be delighted by the easy money. Maybe she'd suggest Natalie. The blonde hadn't been herself since admitting to being in love with a married man who was seventeen years her senior. It would do Natalie good to spend some time with someone fun-loving and easygoing like Amos.

The bidding on a ten-day holiday on the Greek Islands commenced and Scarlet's introspection faded as she lost herself in the electric atmosphere. The holiday and each successive item sold for far more than their worth and she speculated whether people were bidding only to outdo one another and show off their wealth.

But it wasn't until the bidding started for the final item, the performance from Frankenstein's Blood, that her senses prickled. The hairs on the back of her neck lifted even before she turned and locked eyes with a man standing at the back of the room.

Mackenzie.

Her pulse fluttered as his dark, almost black eyes burned into hers. A potent mix of primal need and stark obsession. It was everything she felt for him and then some ... the same everything that had scared her away.

Her belly clenched. Her nipples tightened. Heat swept through her, no doubt flushing her pale-as-pale skin.

"Are you sure everything's okay?" Amos asked, his breath warm on her ear as he leaned close.

Mackenzie's eyes narrowed, a muscle jerking into life in his cheek before she tore her stare away and focused on Amos. "That's the second time you've had to ask me that." She managed a smile. "I'll have to give you a refund at this rate."

Amos grinned, leaning close to whisper, "Believe me, you're worth every cent. Groupies aren't my only concern."

So he'd had a girlfriend or mistress he no longer wanted around? She didn't ask; it was none of her business. She'd learned to listen to her clients, not ask questions. It was part of her service.

The bidding escalated quickly, every man and his dog seemingly wanting the band to play for them. Only when the figures had exceeded even the deepest pockets, and the bidding had died down, did she hear the all too familiar voice at the back of the room.

"Two million."

Amos lifted a bemused brow. "Wouldn't have picked that suited guy for a fan."

She couldn't even smile. Not this time. Few people saw past Mackenzie's business persona. Few people saw the pain he carried around inside him. A pain that seemed only to ease in the bedroom.

The gavel signified Mackenzie's win, and a hush fell over the room when Mackenzie nodded and strode forward to meet the band. At the front row his stare brushed over her before he introduced himself to the band members and shook their hands. "I believe you guys can play at any time, yes?"

Amos nodded. "That's right. We've cleared it with our label. We're free for the next two weeks."

Mackenzie nodded, satisfied. "Then you'll play for this audience, now."

Amos was taken aback. "Seriously?"

Mackenzie had always surprised her, but right then she was lost for words. Two million dollars for an impromptu performance? It was beyond excessive.

"It's for a good cause," he murmured, his gaze moving over her like a caress.

She swallowed hard, mesmerised by him, despite ... everything.

Then he turned back to Amos and the band members, and she could breathe again.

"I couldn't be more serious." Mackenzie paused a beat, and then asked, "You have your gear with you, yes?"

They nodded, and a bearded member of the group said, "We never leave home without it. Everything we need is stashed in my van."

Amos cocked an eyebrow. "Well then, boys. Guess we'd better get this show on the road."

She smiled at Amos when he looked at her, before she said, "I'll wait for you here."

He nodded, and pushed through the crowd. She didn't turn to watch him leave. Not when every cell was attuned to Mackenzie. God, even had she wanted to run away, her trembling legs couldn't have supported her.

Not that she wanted to run. Far from it. She wanted to sit and drink in the man she'd been dreaming about for too long already. The man she'd pretended she didn't have feelings for, since the moment he'd taken more than a strictly business interest in her.

He'd recently had a haircut, the dark brown of his hair cropped close to his head. His cheekbones looked starker, almost angular, as though he'd lost his appetite. Then again, she supposed earning the big money came at a price. He worked hard and slept little.

He played even harder.

"Why are you doing this?" she asked.

His jaw hardened. "I need time alone with you. And if this is the only way I can get it, then so be it."

Her mouth dried. She shouldn't want this, but she did. She wanted it with everything she had.

"Scarlet," he finally acknowledged, her name sounding like a sexual promise and causing the whole world to fade around them, as though no-one else was near.

"Mack," she said softly, reverting to his nickname and unable to formulate even half a word more.

"You look stunning." His eyes flared. "Nothing's changed."

She dragged back her voice. "And I guess that's a compliment."

"One that I'm sure you receive every day from any number of men."

He hated that she was with other men. Yet another reason she couldn't see him anymore. She chewed her bottom lip. Her throat burned, along with the back of her eyes as all her repressed emotions threatened to burst free. "You know how I feel."

Liar. You might tell him you don't return his feelings, but how long will that hold up?

He sighed raggedly. "Yeah, I do." He bent and cupped her chin, his thumb moving back and forth over her lips. "Doesn't mean I have to accept it."

Her belly did a slow flip-flop. "So ... have you? Accepted it, I mean?"

He shook his head. "No, Scarlet, I haven't. Though Lord only knows I've tried."

The man in the red bow tie climbed onto the stage where the auction had been held. The moment he announced that Frankenstein's Blood was going to play, noise erupted around them, cheers and excited chatter that barely infiltrated Scarlet's mind.

She was too busy staring at Mackenzie. In that moment, all her social graces had been left behind. She should stand too, anything to try and wrest back some kind of advantage.

But then his thumb moved to trace over her bottom lip. He bent his head, his voice in her ear sending goose bumps down her spine. "It nearly killed me to see another man kiss you."

She closed her eyes. Little wonder Mackenzie had been front and center in her head tonight. She'd been attuned to him because he'd been in the same room, watching her with Amos. She forced her eyes back open. "It nearly killed me knowing you were with Brandy," she admitted huskily.

His eyes darkened. "You didn't want me."

Her chest ached. I did ... oh, how I did. But I had to protect myself.

His stare softened. "Brandy's beautiful. But she's not you. Not even close."

Scarlet smiled. Brandy—Kate—was still beautiful even after having twin boys a month earlier. Kate no longer worked at the agency, and Scarlet couldn't be happier for her. Kate truly deserved her devoted husband and happily-ever-after.

But no one was irreplaceable. With Kate now gone, Scarlet, along with Tiffany and Savannah, had taken the gorgeous new call girl, Anna—who'd adopted the working name of Candy—under their wing. Inviting her to their lunches and shopping outings, and giving advice whenever she needed some. Anna, with all her innocence ... Scarlet wasn't looking forward to the day she saw the young woman's eyes harden.

The band set up their equipment and began a prerequisite warm up, plucking guitar strings and running through a sound check. She pulled free from Mackenzie's clasp and dragged her eyes away to focus on Amos.

She'd thrown out the rule book tonight. Amos was her client and she was all but rejecting him. She couldn't afford to piss him off and risk ruining her call girl reputation. Not if she wanted to continue supporting her twin sisters, Danni and Tina.

With their mother dead and buried, and their father a distant memory, it'd fallen on her shoulders to keep her sisters clothed, fed and educated. A twinge of resentment flared, and then died away. She'd do anything for the twins. Anything to make sure they had careers they loved, careers that weren't in the sex industry. Careers that were safe and even a little bit predictable.

Mackenzie's eyes narrowed. But whatever he was about to say died in the ruckus immediately after Amos introduced himself and the crowd surged forward.

Scarlet stood, her attention staying on Mackenzie as she shouted above the noise, "I can never be what you want."

As the band broke into sound, she pushed past Mackenzie and headed toward the exit.

"Scarlet, wait!"

She made it to just outside the auditorium before Mackenzie caught her arm and spun her around. His eyes blazed. "I'm not letting you go. Not this time."

She stared up at him, her emotions bubbling over. "I'm not sure I even want you to," she admitted. "Not tonight."

He kissed her then, with more desperate hunger and skill than she could bear. She barely noticed him lifting her against his chest and carrying her away from the noise. She was lost in the kiss, revelling in sensation.

Even guilt over leaving Amos faded away, just the same as Amos's honeyed, baritone voice did when Mackenzie stepped into a room and kicked shut its door. The quiet seemed almost as loud when he turned her around and pressed her back against a wall, his big male body surrounding hers.

She was glad of the shadowy room, where light from the corridor outside was the only illumination to chase away complete darkness. She didn't want him to read her face. Didn't want him to know exactly how much she wanted him.

She was already wet for him, her body a willing recipient to whatever he desired. One touch and she was his. One kiss and she was lost. Lord help her, one last time in his arms, and then she'd walk away from him for good.

He slid his zipper down with a rasp before he undid a button, his pants then dropping low, followed by his underwear. He didn't bother to step out of them. There was too much urgency, too much heat.

With quick, economical movements, he unwrapped a foil from his pocket, and rolled the condom onto his straining shaft. Her heart rate bucked when he lifted her dress and slid aside her lacy thong, then one-handed his cock to center it at her core.

She was hazily aware this sexual encounter was wrong on too many levels, but she didn't much care. She wanted this. Needed this.

His eyes glinted above hers about the same time he drove forward, burying himself deep inside her. Her breath hissed sharply at the pleasure–pain. He'd always been big, always stretched her to the limit. Yet her body readily accepted his impressive length and breadth, readily accepted any of his sexual demands.

She didn't need to pretend sex with this man was wonderful. Not when being with him felt all kinds of right. Not when her every nerve ending burned in his presence, and then exploded the moment they joined.

With his deliberately slow pumps in and out, she was already heading toward the place only Mackenzie knew how to take her. Then he abruptly pulled out, spun her around and leaned her against a huge table. A staff room table, she realized hazily.

His knee between her legs caused her to part them. Then he leaned over her and guided his cock once more between the petals of her labia. "Does your client make you feel this good?" he asked harshly.

She gasped as he entered her then in one long stroke, a hand bunching in her hair and bringing her head back.

"Does he know how you love being taken from behind? How you love your hair pulled just like this?"

"No." Her voice cracked, and she felt his smirk, before his mouth latched onto the side of her neck and his strokes in and out increased until nothing could stop the freight train of an orgasm from ripping through her and tossing her high.

Mackenzie let out a guttural moan as her inner muscles clamped him tight, and he too came, her scalp burning as his hand tightened momentarily, before releasing her.

She was still sucking in breaths from her dizzying ride when he pulled free, disposed of the condom, and then turned her around to face him. "This isn't the end between us, Scarlet," he murmured huskily. His expression might be shadowed, but she sensed his intensity. "It's just the beginning."

If you would like to know when my next book is available, news, cover reveals and more, you can sign up for my newsletter: madmimi.com/signups/121695/join

Check out my website – http://www.melteshco.com/

You can also friend me on Facebook at https://www.facebook.com/mel.teshco

Or on my author Facebook page at https://www.facebook.com/MelTeshcoAuthor

And occasionally on Twitter at https://twitter.com/melteshco

Contact me: melteshco@yahoo.com.au

If you enjoy my books I'd be delighted if you would consider leaving a review. This will help other readers find my books.

## About the Author

Mel Teshco loves to write scorching sci-fi and contemporary stories with an occasional paranormal thrown into the mix. Not easy with seven cats, two dogs and a fat black thoroughbred vying for attention, especially when Mel's also busily stuffing around on Facebook. With only one daughter now living at home to feed two minute noodles, she still shakes her head at how she managed to write with three daughters and three stepchildren living under the same roof. Not to mention Mr. Semi-Patient (the one and same husband hoping for early retirement...he's been waiting a few years now.) Clearly anything is possible, even in the real world.

The VIP Desire Agency: series order
Lady in Red (book 1)
High Class (book 2)
Exclusive (book 3)
Liberated (book 4)
Uninhibited (book 5)
The VIP Desire Boxed Set (all 5 books in the series)
The Virgin Hunt Games volume 1
The Virgin Hunt Games volume 2
The Virgin Hunt Games volume 3
Coming soon
The Virgin Hunt Games volumes 4-6
Alien Hunger: series order
Galactic Burn (book 1)
Galactic Inferno (book 2)
Galactic Flame (book 3)
Coming soon
Galactic Blaze (book 4)
Nightmix: series order:
Lusting the Enemy (book 1)
Abducting the Princess (book 2)
Seducing the Huntress (book 3)
Dragons of Riddich: series order:
Kadin (free prequel - book 1)
Asher (book 2)
Baron (book 3)
Dahlia (book 4)
Wyatt (book 5)
Valor (book 6)
The Queen (book 7)
Winged & Dangerous: series order
Stone Cold Lover (book 1)

Ice Cold Lover (book 2)

Red Hot Lover (book 3)

Winged & Dangerous Box Set (all 3 books in the series)

Box sets with authors Christina Phillips & Cathleen Ross (Kindle Unlimited):

Taken by the Sheikh

Taken by the Billionaire

Taken by the Desert Sheikh

Resisting the Firefighter

Dirty Sexy Space continuity with authors Shona Husk and Denise Rossetti:

Yours to Uncover (book 1)

Mine to Serve (book 6)

Ours to Share (book 8)

Standalone longer length titles: (50k-100k)

Mutant Unveiled

Shadow Hunter

Highest Bid

As I Am

Existence

Standalone novellas and short stories: (15k-35K)

Identity Shift

Moon Thrall

Blood Chance

Carnal Moon

Stripped

Clarissa

Camilla

Selena's Bodyguard (also part of the Christmas Assortment Box)

Anthologies:

Down and Dusty: The Complete Collection

The Christmas Assortment Box

Secret Confessions: Sydney Housewives
Coming soon from December 2021: (KU and Pre-order)
The Sheikh's Runaway Bride
The Sheikh's Captive Lover